Where
Dragons Follow

RETURN OF THE MALEVIR

SUSAN BASS MARCUS
WHERE DRAGONS FOLLOW

Susan is a writer and artist in puppetry and other media. Her stories and novels explore the worlds of "What-If" and "It-Could-Happen-Here."

www.malevir.com

Where Dragons Follow

RETURN OF THE MALEVIR

SUSAN BASS MARCUS

WHERE DRAGONS FOLLOW: RETURN OF THE MALEVIR

ISBN: 978-1-7321434-0-1

Book design by Sarah E. Holroyd (http://sleepingcatbooks.com)
Cover image by Ginger Snap Dragon Studio
Map and interior illustrations by the author

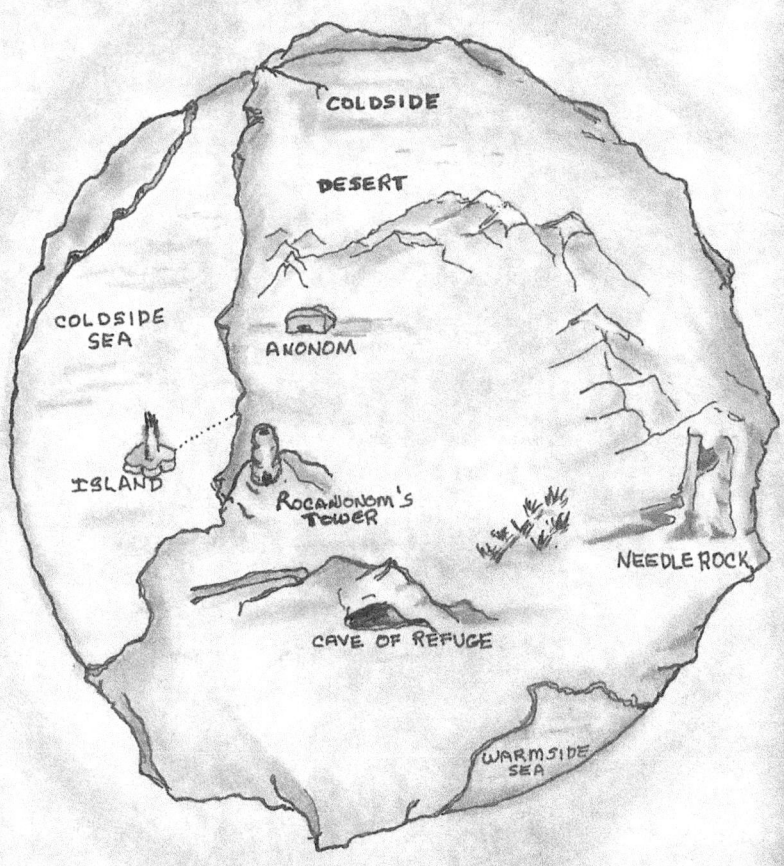

COLDSIDE

DESERT

COLDSIDE
SEA

ANONOM

ISLAND

ROCANONOM'S
TOWER

NEEDLE ROCK

CAVE OF REFUGE

WARMSIDE
SEA

DRAGONWOLDER

FOR STEPHEN, MOLLEE, AND BEN

ACKNOWLEDGMENTS

Professionals in the craft of writing helped me realize this work. Thanks to Stephanie Marshall Ward for her insightful editing; Sarah Holroyd for formatting this final version and pulling it together; and Juliann Crowther for the dazzling cover art.

Thanks also to my many friends and associates who encouraged me to continue the Malevir saga: The Union League Club of Chicago's Writers' Group; the Facebook group ScribesAndBibliophiles; and all those people who cheered me on, in person and online.

Above all, cheers to Stephen, Mollee, and Ben whose support and enthusiasm buoy me up and push me forward.

TABLE OF CONTENTS

Prologue

The Cold Season

Fossarelick, a village of Dragonwolder

STRADDLING A THREE-LEGGED STOOL, Alana watches her brother Kurnan facing her from the edge of his cot. He turns away from her, pulls a coverlet over his head, and curls into himself. As usual, he hides his face from the light.

Alana looks up at the sound of her dragon's voice. Velvet waves caress her thoughts. She returns the call. "Isabella, where are you? I'm in my parents' cottage. Kurnan's sulking in the corner again."

I am with the others in our cave.

"Have you heard Kurnan's thoughts?"

He's shut me out. I feel a hint of his pain and fear, but nothing else.

"He raves when I say your name."

You are my rider now, and you and I have work to do. Come back to the lodge.

"But I worry Kurnan might hurt himself. He's never been the same since surviving the Malevir's attack, and it's getting worse..."

I know. I was there.

"Of course. Sorry. I hate this sickness in his body and spirit."

A nightmare clings to him.

Alana does not answer.

What happened? I can't hear your thoughts either, Alana.

"I'm safe. I was looking for my cloak. This Cold-Turn is terrible. That dark orb blocks our sun's faint light, and the gloom doesn't help Kurnan's mood, I tell you."

The fields froze over far too soon.

"At night, I can see the moon reflected on their icy surface."

We've had Cold-Turns before, but not like this.

"I remember, during the last Warm-Turn, ragged tendrils of mist rolling across the land. They snagged on trees and caught on mountain crags surrounding our Veiled Valley, shrouded as it often is—or was—in fog and drizzle. These days, all we see is snow and ice."

Alana shivers. It's hard to forget the Malevir who rose from those mists so long ago. Who destroyed valley settlements and burned fields. Who maimed and killed livestock belonging to her neighbors and family.

"Why did the Malevir kill your dragon kin, Isabella? Thank the Ways of the World some of you survived his attacks."

I'll explain when you return to the lodge. Shall I come for you?

"Not just yet." Alana looks toward Nnylf and Azile's cottage. Not so long ago, they had joined dragons in battling the Malevir. Their mother, a dragonrider, had trained them all for the battle to reclaim the Veiled Valley. "I need to stay here with Kurnan. He's been ill ever since you last saw him. He doesn't even know we beat the Malevir."

It was not the Malevir we defeated, but his tool, the aiglonax, a terrible beast. This strange cold season and the dark orb are signs he never left.

"Hmm. Yes, I suppose you're right. When we last flew together, I saw odd cloud formations and peculiar sinkholes scattered across the valley. We're all a bit edgy. Even you and Draako fret more these days."

I remember when the Malevir came to Dragonwolder. We thought he was a demon dragonrider because he killed his mount, the Golden Dragon Lustredust.

"I didn't hear that story, but Azile saw him shift into a hork too." She cringes remembering the smelly blue-green ogre, nothing compared to the form the Malevir took when Isabella battled him: Aindle, a horrible two-headed aiglonax—the creature that poisoned Kurnan.

Makes me sick.

"Do you think Kurnan ever thinks about you, dear Isabella? Does he look out the window, at that heavy gray sky and our dim sun, and remember flying with you?"

Alana feels, rather than hears, Isabella's sigh. She glances out the window at the blot covering much of the sun's face. It hovers over Dragonwolder as if waiting for someone, locking the valley in an endless winter. Dark clouds are scudding above the wind-chilled land, like a reflection of her brother's moods. She misses the warm season and her dragon friends. Battling the Malevir drained most of them.

"Where are my dragon friends now?"

Alana, most of them are hibernating. The Cave of the Ancestors, our ancient home, shelters them from the cold, all except Draako, Ruddykin, and Aurykk.

"So nearly every valley creature I know has a quiet, restful life, snug inside thick-walled cottages, caves, or burrows. But not you. Not I, and certainly not Kurnan."

Isabella's grief floods Alana's body.

To change the subject, Alana asks, "And where is our valley's oldest and wisest dragon?"

Aurykk lives in the Cave of Refuge, very much awake and probably worried about the Malevir.

"Where's that cave?"

On the sunsetside edge of the Veiled Valley. I imagine he's easing into his old age with long naps and good food.

"Yes, I'm sure he has plenty of tasty gems in his treasure hoard, sweetened by a steady supply of mice."

We need you and Nnylf back at the lodge.

"I can't leave Kurnan just now."

Well, Nnylf and Draako need to practice more. Where is Nnylf?

"Here in Fossarelick." Alana smiles as she recalls Nnylf riding Draako, the gorgeous Silver Dragon who chose him as his dragon-rider. "Remember when he and Draako were young and they bonded while fighting dragon wraiths? I must admit Nnylf shares some of Draako's best traits, like bravery." She thought about Nnylf's high cheekbones and large brown eyes. "Maybe I think about Nnylf too much."

No, but you and Kurnan were happy before we dragons chose you.

"We grew up with Nnylf and Azile in Fossarelick. All of us worked the fields with our parents and spent evenings around our hearths, scaring each other with tales of fierce dragons—"

Little knowing how much your lives soon would depend on us.

Alana is silent for a moment. When the dragons returned to the valley and chose her, Kurnan, Nnylf, and Azile to be their riders, their lives became something they couldn't have imagined. All four of them became the stuff of legends—until the aiglonax poisoned Kurnan.

From under his covers, Kurnan is screaming at Alana. He orders her to leave.

"What can I do, Isabella, when he acts this way? I should go, I guess. I'm tucking the few belongings I need into my sack. You can come for me now."

Alana thinks about soaring above Fossarelick and the valley. When Isabella carries her high over Dragonwolder, everything seems frigid and bleak. Yet, up there, icicle-fringed cottages and farm buildings, scattered across a broad hilltop, look like a toy village surrounded by snow-glazed fields. She often spots friends below, tiny figures busy at their chores. Since Aindle's defeat, no one fears losing a cow or donkey to a dreaded monster's fangs. The beast's firestorms will no longer ravage their crops in the next warm season. Even their friend, the giant Rocánonom who challenged the Malevir's dark magic with his own spells, has retired to his mountaintop tower. She wonders if he ever worries the Malevir will return to Dragonwolder.

"Isabella, I've seen Kurnan's cuts, bruises, and broken bones heal, but I think terrible memories haunt him. Mother says he sleeps in fits and starts. He often wakes up screaming.

"Whenever I visit the cottage, I try to talk to him, but Kurnan always answers my questions with a scowl. If I bring up his dragon-rider days or say your name, he leaves the cottage. The sound of its heavy wooden door slamming behind him shakes me to the bone. I do miss the happy, adventurous boy who was my brother. I wish I could tell my parents Kurnan will find his way back to us, but I can't think of how that will happen."

PART 1

A WAY OUT

KURNAN

HIS BODY WAS WHOLE again but rasping voices and painful memories filled his throbbing head and ruined his sleep. His nightmares, overshadowing his waking life, had him running from a screeching aiglonax's outstretched talons or falling, falling, and never hitting the ground. In the dream that shook him awake his last morning in Fossarelick, strands of strangling mist were snaking around his throat and choking him.

Gasping, Kurnan sat up and flung off his light coverlet. His straw-filled mattress was soggy with sweat. Voices called him and wiped out the remains of his dreams. Kurnan flinched and rubbed his temples. Faint morning light crept under the cottage door and brightened one small window on the wall opposite him. His eyes burned, and he threw the damp coverlet over his head to block the light.

In the dark, he heard the voices' familiar message: *Run away. Forget your shame.* The amulet he wore warmed his chest. Whenever the voices inside his head talked to him, the amulet heated up his skin until it burned, but when he pulled open his tunic and brushed the amulet aside, the searing heat had left no blisters, not even a red mark. Kurnan's days always began this way.

Since he'd stolen the amulet from its hiding place, near Nnylf's family cottage, he could not bear being with people. Even now, he shrank from Mother when she tried to reason with him. "My boy, your dreams are only—well, dreams. The aiglonax's attack hurt you, but that was long ago. Forget the beast. It's dead. Now get up. Dress yourself. Your father needs your help. The brook has frozen over again."

Kurnan glared at his mother, a small bowl of steaming barley porridge in her hands. "Everyone's telling me what to do. Why can't you leave me alone?" Why were people treating him like a child, always saying, "poor Kurnan, poor Kurnan"? He hated their pity.

"I only want you to heal and be happy." She shrugged and held out the bowl. "Eat a little something."

"Eat? That?" He cringed as nausea gripped his stomach. "I'm too tired. Why can't someone else help Father?"

"My poor Kurnan, you're the one he wants. Besides, the work will do you good. It'll help you forget the Malevir. Remember, his powers died with him. Remember, the dragons came back to us. They're friendly."

"No, don't talk of dragons," he mumbled.

"What did you say?"

Kurnan stared at his feet, making little hills under the coverlet. He knew his mother was looking at him but said nothing more. He waved away the food she offered. He lay again on his cot, turned to face the wall, and pulled the coverlet over his head. He heard his mother sigh as her footsteps reached the hearth. He did not want to tell her about the voices. They swarmed in his head until their noise grew painful.

One of those voices called to him the moment his mother walked out of the cottage. *Kurnan, why stay here? Get up.*

"No, go away!" he shouted, tossing aside the covers. He shook his fist toward the loft.

Kurnan, you can't stay.

"Why should I leave?" His words dwindled to a whisper.

To end your pain.

Kurnan sat up again and looked around the dim room. His parents' bed stood in the opposite corner, next to a high wooden chest and cupboard. When he was much younger, his mother used to carry him, trembling, from his cot and settle him in her warm bed between herself and his father. They would hug and soothe him. Childhood's bad dreams could not compare to the night terrors that attacked him now, reminders of the aiglonax's poison, suffocating green vapor, and unrelenting pain and sickness.

My amulet protects you.

Kurnan groaned and rubbed the back of his aching head.

Leave Fossarelick. That pain will end.

Today's voice echoed in Kurnan's skull. He knew it came neither from his parents' corner nor from the loft where Alana once slept and kept her belongings. Several World-Turns ago, she and Nnylf had accepted work at the Protectors' Lodge across the Veiled Valley, far from home. Mother and Father missed her, but Kurnan did not. If everyone would leave him alone and stop trying to help him, he'd be fine.

"I can't leave," he told the voice. "I have nothing and nowhere to go."

We have a place for you. We will provide.

Kurnan wiped tears from his cheeks and rubbed his eyes. "No, no, if I go, what will happen to me? They'll come looking for me."

We will show you the way. We will hide you. No one knows you have my amulet.

Kurnan's pulse quickened. *No one knows? Of course, no one knows.*

Stand up, Kurnan. Forget the aiglonax.

Kurnan threw his legs over the side of the cot and, lightheaded, staggered around the room. The memory of aiglonax poisons made him weak and queasy.

Dress yourself. Put on your boots.

Shaking, he took some time to pull his boots over warm leggings and tighten the ties that bound his cloak. He bent over the hearth and stuck his fingers into the bowl of porridge Mother had left for him. As he licked his fingers, strength returned to his legs. The thick cereal comforted his belly.

The voice called again.

Kurnan, take your mother's sack from the cupboard.

Kurnan obeyed without question, relieved that the jabbing pains were ebbing. He trudged to the cupboard and pulled out a homespun brown sack.

You'll need dried meats and grain, a hammer and other tools, and your coverlet.

He found some jerky, a small pouch of grain, another with seeds, and a few tools his father would not miss. He stuffed them into the sack. The rolled-up blue coverlet followed, plus extra leggings, a woolen tunic, some hard biscuits, and a pot.

Don't forget your flint box and your cap.

After strapping the large sack to his back, Kurnan left the cottage and closed the door without making a sound. He set off down the hill along a path hidden by tall, prickly gorse bushes. He was sure no one saw him leave.

DRAAKO

HEAVY FOOTFALLS ECHOED IN the Cave of the Ancestors as a dragon paced around stalactites hanging from the ceiling. His silvery scales rippled with every stride. Indigo patches dotted the dragon's powerful legs and the bowed spikes running from his neck frill to the tip of his tail. He ducked under the cave's arched opening and stood outside on a broad ledge. As he viewed the Veiled Valley below and the mountains beyond, he called to Nnylf, *Where are you?* He shook his long head when his rider did not answer. Blue smoke escaped in curlicues through gaps between his protruding fangs. *Nnylf, no need to fly today. Everything is quiet in Dragonwolder.*

Do you hear me, Draako?

Draako turned, surprised at the sound of his name. A different voice, not Nnylf's, but Isabella's. He trotted back inside the cave.

Draako, we're in the lair. Ruddykin has news.

I hope it's not bad news. I could use a nap.

Silence.

He exhaled more tendrils of smoke as he entered a high-vaulted chamber and slid into a cool, black pool that spanned the floor. A whirlpool sucked him down through the water and dropped him gently onto broad, dry slabs of limestone. Then the water rose far over his head and lay even with the floor of the chamber above.

Many strides beyond him, at the head of a dark tunnel leading away from the slabs, was a familiar mound of shimmering treasure. Perched on the glowing mound, an upright and agitated Red Dragon belched cinders and shouted, "We face a new threat to Dragonwolder and our Scintilla!"

Beside Ruddykin the Red sat Draako's cousin, Isabella. Her russet scales glistened in the Scintilla's dazzling beams. Licking her foreleg, Isabella paused when she saw Draako approaching the mound. "The Scintilla's glow is warm and strong today, but..."

"But?"

"Its power and ours might be in danger."

"Can't be that bad. We've seen the last of the Malevir."

"Maybe yes, maybe no. If the beast should find the Scintilla..." She shrugged. The Malevir had tried many times to steal the Mystic Scintilla, source of dragon fire and reason.

She turned to Ruddykin. "I can't hide it any longer. Shall I tell him?"

The Red Dragon nodded.

Isabella faced Draako and continued, "Some think the Malevir has returned to Dragonwolder. There! I've said it."

"And, Draako," added Ruddykin, "while Nnylf was in Fossarelick, he looked for the Malevir's amulet in its hiding place, where he hoped to keep it from harming anyone."

"And?"

"What do you mean 'and?' Didn't he tell you?" Ruddykin grumbled and belched a glob of cinders.

"No, we, well, I..."

Isabella, coughing a murky cloud of ashes, explained. "Draako and Nnylf have not been flying much these days. Tell him what happened."

"Nnylf couldn't find the amulet. Anywhere. It must have been missing for quite a while. Why didn't Nnylf tell you?"

"We...er...we haven't been making our practice flights."

"Why?"

"Er, since the Cold-Turn grew bitter, I...we...haven't needed to... well, maybe a flight or two—"

Isabella cut him off. "Careless of you. Both of you. You are Protectors and that's your job." She paused and stared at the mound. "Ruddykin cannot leave the lair to chase the thief. He is Guardian of the Scintilla." She glared at Draako. "All the other dragons rest in Cold-Turn sleep. We are the only dragons who can help." She slid off the mound, lowered her steaming snout close to Draako's, and growled. "Alana and I share our thoughts every day. You should do the same with Nnylf. We must be ready to find the amulet thief."

"Thief? Who would want to steal such a dangerous thing? Perhaps the wind picked it up and buried it in a snow dune."

"Unlikely," Isabella snorted. "Somehow the Malevir found a way to worm into it again. We must find it before he uses it against Dragonwolder."

"But the Malevir is dead. We saw him fall apart and turn to dust."

"I do not believe the Malevir is dead." Isabella exhaled a long plume of gray smoke. "We saw only Aindle, his aiglonax, perish. We'd better take care when we fly with our riders. Could be the Malevir has been biding his time, getting angrier—and more dangerous every World-Turn that passes."

"Ha! The Malevir's probably just a mean old dragon hermit, jealous of our strength."

"Pish-tosh. By the way, what's kept you away from Nnylf?"

"I confess my thoughts were elsewhere, with wise, old Aurykk. I miss him. He used to make everything feel calm and right. He's in his Twilight Time and weaker now..." Draako did not know how to talk about his worries. Aurykk was his clan's elder. While all the other dragons were hibernating, he relied on the Golden Dragon for advice and encouragement.

Isabella patted her roughened scales. "I miss my father too, but don't you think Nnylf misses you the same way you miss Aurykk? That he feels protected when you are together? You know Aurykk is warm and well supplied, deep inside the Cave of Refuge. I assure you he's happy and comfortable."

"Yes, the cave is big and full of his favorite gemstones, but maybe he's not as happy as he used to be. At his age...*harum.*" A lump burned in his throat. "At his age, he needs someone to look after him. Patches of his scales are white, and he's fatter around the middle and—"

"Enough!" Ruddykin erupted in a dark, sulfurous cloud. He spread his wings and, flapping them, grazed the ceiling. "Aurykk's powers still outshine our own. He knows more about Dragonwolder than we could ever imagine. He probably planned schemes to thwart the Malevir's return long before today."

A spray of cinders shot from Draako's snout. "Does he think the Malevir really is..."

"Really is what, Draako?"

"Coming back to Dragonwolder?"

"As if the beast ever left! I think he's been here, brooding in Fossarelick."

Isabella coughed a cinder ball. "Maybe Draako should ask Aurykk what we should do."

The Red rose from the mound and roared, "First search the valley for the thief, *then* visit Aurykk, share what you have learned, and listen to his advice." Ruddykin hopped off the mound. A brilliant shaft of light shot past him and hit the chamber's roof. Jagged quartz crystals crumbled into sparkling, floating dust motes. They settled on the giant Red's crimson scales, coating his glistening snout, ears, and frill. He stretched his wings. "As long as Nnylf kept the amulet buried, he weakened the Malevir's power, but now who knows what will happen? If I could leave here, I'd hunt it down and destroy it for good, but…"

"But that's *our* task." Draako's scales rippled. He stood tall on his back legs. "To the lodge, then?"

Isabella nodded. "We will survey the valley. After that, Draako, you will report to Aurykk. He'll invite you into his lair for a nice long chat, and you won't worry so much about him. Call Nnylf. Share our plans."

Draako pressed his fangs into his lower lip, bowed his head, and sent his message: *Nnylf, I'm coming for you. We're going to look for the amulet.*

ALANA

NNYLF'S BAD NEWS GAVE Alana a headache. All Fossarelick suspected her brother had taken the amulet since both disappeared at the same time, well before Nnylf discovered it was missing. "Maybe they're wrong. Maybe Kurnan is looking for us," Nnylf suggested, "and it's just a coincidence."

Alana shook her head. "Kind words, Nnylf, but Kurnan's not looking for us, believe me." She looked into her friend's dark brown eyes and enjoyed the shiver of happiness that ran through her whenever he was near. "But I don't understand why Kurnan would take that piece of rubbish you found in the aiglonax's ashes. It didn't protect the aiglonax." She paused and her voice caught in her throat. She whispered, "If Kurnan did take the amulet, I think the Malevir made him do it."

"The Malevir? He's dead. No, this is all my fault. Any trinket of the Malevir's carries some of the beast's power. I should have left it with Rocánonom." Nnylf reached out to pat her shoulder, but Alana, her body knotted with worry, stepped aside.

"It's no one's fault," she muttered as she paced the room. "My fever-crazed brother is wandering again. His sickness has returned, worse than ever. We must find him. Amulet or no amulet."

Alana sighed. Once more, she had to rescue her brother from himself. She pictured their beautiful Copper Dragon, sunlight burnishing her scales as she flew above the clouds. Alana called to her. *Isabella, my friend, Kurnan has left Fossarelick and we must look for him.*

Nnylf poked Alana's elbow. "Sorry, I forgot to tell you Draako brought me back here."

In the next instant, Isabella's answer danced in their thoughts. *We know. I am gliding into the lodge clearing now. Meet Draako and me there.*

༄

Before leaving the lodge's main hall, Alana reminded Nnylf to dress for the cold. They slipped dragonrider armor over layers of woolens, flung on cloaks, and hurried through a large doorway. A garden, buried in snow, surrounded the broad stone lodge and its graceful tower. They crossed it and, clomping through rows of gnarled and frozen apple trees, reached the edge of an ice-glazed clearing.

A stark and leafless forest loomed over the clearing where two waiting dragons crouched. Alana ran to Isabella and rubbed her dragon's steaming snout. Isabella extended a leg. Alana climbed up and felt herself relax as Isabella's copper scales warmed her chilled hands. She settled herself behind Isabella's neck frill and prepared to fly.

Feeling Isabella's shoulder muscles flex against her legs, Alana stole a glimpse of Nnylf racing up Draako's flank. She noticed how well his chest filled his leather armor. Nnylf had become so strong, and he looked confident and serious settled onto the Silver's neck hump, which had been his seat for so many thrilling flights.

Isabella spoke first. "Ready? Caps covering your ears? Kurnan cannot have traveled far. Ice and snow will slow him."

"Yes," Alana said. "We're ready. Where to?" As the Copper leaped skyward, Alana heard her thoughts. *Anonom Trace, then the River Valley. Kurnan might be wandering coldside, to cross the frozen sea.*

Why the sea?

Don't you know about the island?

Alana's knees twitched. She remembered her father's nightmarish tales of legendary demons said to haunt a sprawling island tower.

I've heard some stories. Alana hoped the others would not hear her thoughts. *Ways of the World, please protect my brother. Why would he go there?* She allowed herself only a glance at the sun, partially blocked by the dark orb hovering over Dragonwolder. Lowering her gaze, she studied the land below them.

Pale blue shadows of the dragons and their riders crossed the snowbound Veiled Valley. They glided into Anonom Trace and landed among the ruins of an ancient village, once prosperous but destroyed by the Malevir before Alana was born. Anonom was locked in the frigid Cold-Turn. Its crumbled lodges and collapsed towers lay deserted and gray in the wan sunlight. Those who used to inhabit Anonom lived elsewhere, hoping to rebuild their village at the end of this wintry cycle.

With a sigh, Alana pulled her long cape more tightly around her slender body and looked at the heavy clouds above them. She was a small part of a world slowly circling one star in a greater universe. Dragonwolder's seasons alternated, warm in one cycle and frigid in the next. This Cold-Turn was unusually long. She imagined Kurnan's feet freezing as he trudged through razor-edged broken snow crust. Worry gripped her, more than the cold that pinched her shoulders.

He's not here, Isabella sang out. *No footprints, everything's perfectly frozen and undisturbed.*

The two riders mounted again and hunched over as heavy winds buffeted them. They were crossing the Sunsetside Mountains and heading toward the River Valley. Strong gusts whipped around the mountains, and sleet pelted Alana's head. She knew the biting cold of this World-Turn made her dragon's wings ache as they beat through the icy air. With one hand on Isabella's frill, Alana pulled her woolen cap back over her ears and ducked her head.

Isabella, can you see anything?

Her dragon was silent. Suddenly, she dived toward the river that wound sunsetside toward the sea. Alana tightened her grip but almost fell off Isabella at the sight of a young man standing on the river's warmside bank. He was pacing back and forth.

Call him, Isabella. That's Kurnan. Tell him to stop.

I am. I am. He does not hear me, and I cannot hear his thoughts. Truly, he has forgotten me.

Alana could feel Isabella's grief. A sharp pain started in her chest and wracked her body. *Isabella, please be calm. Your pain hurts me so.*

Alana, how can I save him?

Can we catch him and carry him away?

Not if he is the one who stole the amulet.

Draako interrupted. *Alana, you and Isabella must hurry to Rocánonom's eyrie and warn him. He will use magick to keep your brother far from the sea. If Kurnan crosses the ice, he will reach the island and I fear—*

Fear what?

Danger. That is all I can say. Will you go? Now?

Isabella's grief eased, and Alana's body relaxed. *Yes, we're ready now. And you?*

Nnylf and I will find Aurykk.

Nnylf nodded and waved goodbye as Draako flew toward the Cave of Refuge, on the other side of the mountain peaks. Her teeth chattering, Alana waved back and watched Draako carry him away.

ROCÁNONOM

STANDING AT THE EDGE of a cliff, Rocánonom scanned the Coldside Sea far below. Frozen waves fixed the shoreline in a broken-toothed grin. Ice floes butted against each other, some slipping under the weight of the glacial calves that rammed them. Anyone daring enough—or driven by demons—could cross the sea by leaping from one ice floe to the next. The wizardly giant frowned and, turning inland, he muttered a string of incantations. Perhaps those spells would blunt the wintry blasts battering the land.

Tugging a knitted wool cap over his thick auburn curls and raw, reddened ears, Rocánonom climbed the steep slope up to his shelter, a stone tower built on a mountain crag. With long and powerful strides, he circled his home. After every few steps, he paused. Cupping one ear, he waited for the sound of his messenger's approach. He heard only the wind's piercing whistle as it whipped around his tower.

Shrugging in disappointment, the giant trudged to his door and shoved it open with his shoulder. With only a glance at his high-ceilinged hall and the low hearth in the middle of the stone floor, Rocánonom hung his cap and heavy cloak on a peg near the door. He rubbed his chill-whitened hands and tucked them into his armpits.

The moment his fingers felt warmth seep through his woolen tunic, he took a long, scorched stick and poked the dying fire in his hearth, reviving it with clumps of dry moss. Time for a warm drink. The old way. He boiled water in a pot then mixed it with thick cider syrup from a silver beaker. No sense wasting his magick to warm the brew. No good comes from offending the Ways of the World. He needed Their blessing now.

While sipping soothing draughts of cider, Rocánonom carried a three-legged stool closer to the hearth and sat. He stretched his legs and drained the rest of his drink. He remained by the hearth for so long, without moving, that the fire began to smoke and die away again. Coughing, the giant threw on more moss, then he pulled a note out of his vest and reread it:

> Rocánonom—may the Ways of the World guide
>   and protect you.
> They have not been so kind to Fossarelick.
> Kurnan stole the amulet. Do not let him reach
>   the Sea.
> Isabella cannot stop him.
> I shall send word when I know more.
>
> —Sweetnettle

As Rocánonom read, he gagged. Cider gurgled from his belly and burned his throat. "Great Forces above and below, you strengthened me when the valley folk needed me to fight the Malevir. Where are you now? Please, help me. Kurnan must not reach the sea." He thanked the Ways of the World for his loyal friend Sweetnettle. The Lobli sprite had faced the Malevir many times in the past and nearly died for it.

Against the wall near a winding stone staircase sat a long table.

Rocánonom unrolled a scroll lying there and studied the drawings and script that covered its surface. Closing his eyes, he rehearsed a few phrases then stood at one of the tower's small mottled windows. Looking outside, he stretched an arm in the direction of the Coldside Sea. He chanted the phrases, which echoed from the tower walls, rearranging themselves into a different sequence. After the echoes died away, he heard the wind rise and change its tune. Through the window, Rocánonom could see melting jade-green waves arch and roll toward the sea's rocky shoreline.

The Elementals, dragon-sourced energies, were at work. At first, wispy clouds drifted over the seashore. As if they were caught in a brilliant sunset, they turned crimson. Massing, they took the form of immense dragons and joined each other, head to tail, until they formed a whirling circle. The heat they radiated began to soften the landscape. The frozen river's surface shattered into massive melting ice floes.

"If only Nnylf had trusted the dragons or me with the amulet, instead of pocketing it and hiding it all these many World-Turns," Rocánonom muttered. "How *did* Kurnan find the amulet and run away with it?" He regretted not doing more to remove the amulet's power. Left alone for so long, the Malevir had time to strengthen it and use it to control whoever wore it.

Kurnan must not cross the sea. The Elementals will slow his journey. Melting snow has swollen the river. That will delay him. Maybe stop him? Any delay will give Isabella and Draako time to find him. Rocánonom rubbed the window pane with two fingers, and the ice that clouded it melted away. *But how did Kurnan know about the amulet? Why would he take it? Wouldn't it remind him of the beast that tried to kill him?*

Rocánonom turned away from the window and rubbed his forehead with his enormous hand. *Kurnan is a sad and withdrawn young man. They tell me he hardly speaks with anyone, sunrising to sunset-*

ting. A dragon always hears her rider's thoughts, but Kurnan's ears are shut to Isabella's voice. She no longer feels his heartbeat. Now his sister rides the Copper in his place. How I'd like to see Alana's face again.

Rocánonom studied his cook fire. Little blue-yellow flames ate away at the moss and danced among embers inside the ring of thick raised stones that bordered his hearth. They reminded him of the day he taught a young dragon to use his spark glands and shoot a stream of fire from his mouth and nostrils. The blaze burst through the mouth of the dragon clan's ancestral cave and charred nearly all the vegetation that grew nearby. He laughed then sighed as he remembered the dragons' great feats.

How he admired them all, so powerful, yet so willing to forget past offenses—even bearing the blame for the Malevir's misdeeds—to rebuild their friendship with the Veiled Valley's folk. He also treasured his ties to the Elementals, dragon spirit-beings so powerful that they could interfere with the Great Forces of earth, air, fire, and water.

Rocánonom winced. Would his connection to the Elementals last? Should he waken the dragons from their comfortable Cold-Turn rest to help him strengthen that bond? *If the Malevir's amulet has the power to hide Kurnan from Draako and Nnylf, then that power could endanger all Dragonwolder.*

Smoke billowing from his hearth had him scrounging for more tinder. Its acrid smell scratched his throat and brought back another memory, of the day his brown weasel friends nearly sacrificed themselves. Throughout their battles with Aindle, the weasels knew they had the power to take him down. They waited, almost too long, for the right moment. Just as Aindle froze within a Silver Dragon's Cone of Cold, the weasels jumped into the two-headed aiglonax's open jaws and down his throats. The aiglonax, a nearly invincible form of the Malevir, could not resist the dragons' and weasels' double assault. The beast convulsed and fell. His hissing body parts turned into foul gray ashes. Draako found the cursed amulet in those ashes, but

Nnylf palmed it and hid it away. At least, that's what his fearless little friends the weasels told him before they skittered off to their home in the wilds. As far as Rocánonom knew, they were grooming their white Cold-Turn coats and frolicking along the frozen river beyond the Sunsetside Mountains.

Rocánonom missed their nattering conversation. He was used to laughing in their company. He also missed the tinkling giggles of his Loblin friends, little woodland sprites as caring as house brownies and as daring as wood elves. They'd worked hard to build and care for human settlements. The Malevir's horrible dark magick had enslaved them as goblins and uprooters, but Nnylf and Azile had found a way to free them from their grim goblin life underground. At least Sweetnettle had stayed with him after the other Loblin left to rebuild their nests and tunnels across the valley and under the new towns. Where was Sweetnettle now? Why hadn't he answered Rocánonom's last message?

Through the roar of the wind, Rocánonom heard massive thumps and heavy footsteps crunching through crusty snow. He flung his cloak over his broad shoulders and dashed outside. Filling the terrace in front of his tower, a Copper Dragon and her female rider greeted him with their thoughts. Each wished him well. The young woman was running toward him.

She called out, "Rocánonom, help us stop Kurnan! He is trying to reach the Coldside Sea. We saw him nearing the shore."

"You did see him? Then it is well I summoned an enchantment to stop him, but Alana, dear girl, please come inside and warm yourself. I was hoping to see you. And what may I offer you, Isabella?"

I have my inner flame to warm me, good giant. While you and Alana talk within the shelter of your tower, I will stay on the lee side of the hill. My wings will cover me. Go, Alana. Share what we have learned.

"No, no, my lady," Rocánonom said. "I'd rather you follow the slope to a more protected spot. You know where it is."

The Copper nodded. She left a deep, icy trench behind her as she plodded through snowdrifts then descended to a natural rock shelter facing the valley. Rocánonom watched her settle in. Tonguing a few wriggling green snakes out of her jaw pouch, Isabella spat them onto the gravel-strewn stones. Grunting with satisfaction, she ate all but one, which she rolled into a deep snowdrift just inside the entrance to the shelter. Rocánonom smiled, thinking, *she's saving a tasty tidbit for later.*

KURNAN

THE RIVER WAS FLOODING its banks and running in a torrent. Kurnan slung his sack over the small of his back to save his aching shoulder from the weight of his boots. Sharp stones jabbed his bare feet as he slid across stubs of frosty grasses and weeds near the edge of the river bank.

"I don't know how to do this. Where's the snow? The river should be frozen over."

Turn away.

"Why? You wanted me to reach the sea."

In time. The sea ice is melting. You must find another way.

Kurnan rubbed his temples and stared coldside across the river. "The river will take me to the sea. You promised no more pain when I reached the sea."

Your pain ends soon, but not here.

"I can't..." Kurnan's forehead ached as the voice grew louder.

Go to the Warmside.

He shifted his gaze to the lands behind him. "You want me to go where nothing lives but sawgrass and monsters?"

The valley folk know you have the amulet. Go.

Waves of fear swept through Kurnan, and he could hardly breathe. He backed away from the swollen river until dry ground supported his feet. He sat on the rotted trunk of an old storm-felled tree and laid his sack next to his feet. His blood coursed as madly through his veins as the water that surged in the river beyond him. *They know? But how? If only I could reach the sea.*

He stared into the distance beyond the river. Shards of white light hit his eyes, and his head throbbed as dazzling blue floodwaters coursed over the ice and snow.

Put on your boots. Snow and ice lie between here and the Warmside. Pain ends when you reach the red needlerock.

The amulet began to heat the hollow in Kurnan's neck. He grimaced and shut out the discomfort as he bowed to the change of plans. With little spirit, he pulled his boots out of the sack, and a thick barley cake tumbled to the ground. Kurnan devoured it in a few bites. He pushed aside his other belongings until he found his water gourd and gulped most of its contents. After drying his feet again with the ends of his sash, Kurnan wrapped them in rags. He rolled down his leggings and slipped on his boots. Standing, he adjusted the sack on his shoulder, refilled the gourd with river water, and turned away from the sea.

"I'm going. May the Ways of the World protect me," he whispered as he yanked the amulet out of his tunic. "And, O Ways, stop these voices from haunting my days as well as my nights." Kurnan began his trek to the Warmside.

PART 2

NEW ALLIES

ALANA

JUST BEYOND THE HEARTH'S stone circle, Alana and Rocánonom sat bemused, gazing wordlessly into the fire. Alana was smiling; Rocánonom's presence and his hearth bathed her in warmth and safety. Dried moss and wood crackled under dancing flames while outside a snowstorm whipped around the giant's tower and dimmed the day's remaining light. Alana's hands wrapped around the small jug of warm cider she held close to her chin. She inhaled fragrant steam rising from its rim.

"You've known us since we were children," she said to the giant. "Can you explain my brother's latest foolishness?"

"Foolishness? Why do you say that?"

Alana's frown deepened. "Sometimes he talks to the air. He squeezes the sides of his head and screams, 'Shut up!'"

"Why is that 'foolishness'?"

"The first time he did that, I thought he was screaming at me. I was in the loft and hadn't said a word. I came down. He wasn't even aware I was standing in front of him."

Rocánonom sat for a while, his thick forefinger pressed to his lips. Then he placed his jug next to the hearth. "Alana, some beings or spirits *are* there, are talking to him, but only Kurnan can hear them. They infected him when he breathed the aiglonax's poison. If he has taken the amulet, as you say, they..." The giant shook his head. "If he were only wandering, I'd..."

"You'd do what?" Alana coughed and spilled her cider on the hot stones. The droplets sizzled as she looked up at the giant's sad face. "Tell me."

"You said your brother seemed determined to reach the Coldside Sea. Why?"

Alana chewed her lower lip. "I don't know. Where would he go? Not to the island, surely? Isn't that just a story?"

Picking up his jug, Rocánonom invited Alana to join him next to the massive oaken tabletop covered by stacks of scrolls. The giant unrolled one of them. He asked her to hold down one edge while his jug anchored the other. He smoothed the parchment until Alana could see all the drawings that filled it. There was the Veiled Valley, enclosed on three sides by mountains. Up top sat the Coldside Desert and its basilisk plunge holes. Closer to the left edge of the scroll and far beyond the Sunsetside Mountains, she made out the jagged shore of the Coldside Sea.

Rocánonom placed his broad thumb on a spot in the middle of the sea. When he lifted it, Alana recognized the outlines of a large island, dominated by a tower. Whoever had drawn the map had shown the tower was quite high, surrounding its upper third with clouds.

"Is this the tower where they say only dark spirits dwell? Who drew this map?"

Rocánonom gazed past her, through the window. "You've heard the stories, I see. I drew the map to remember my journey, long, long ago, across that vast sea. I stopped on the island to rest, well before I made my home in the Trace. I was one of three giants who wandered throughout the Beyond at the end of a wintry World-Turn. The Ways of the World called all of us, from our different realms, to journey toward the greening plains of the Veiled Valley. We were to find each other and prepare the land for its new human inhabitants—your ancestors among them. We would become their Guardians—Protectors of the Trace, the Forest, and the Mountains—and we would serve as the dragons' aides.

"I came from the Edge of Beyond on the far side of the sea. I remember the other two, both struggling under an enchantment I had escaped. Haldoren, the second giant, was gruff and twisted, his skin rough as tree bark. The Ways of the World had called him from the High Beyond. To reach the Veiled Valley, he had to cross the Coldside Desert.

"The third giant, my extraordinary friend Enderfon, trekked from the Low Beyond into the Warmside. He carried a weapon filled with immense power, a mace he called Rowel. I can still picture his smiles and rough-hewn blue cheeks, rounded like sea-tossed boulders. He wasn't always a rock giant, but he bravely endured the spell that made him such.

"Only one of us survived the journey, I think. Brave Haldoren dodged the many basilisk pits and nests that pocked the desert sands, but they say an aiglonax ambushed him. Swooping down from the mountains, it grasped my friend in its talons, tore him in two, and devoured him—or so the Loblin told me.

"Enderfon faced a different foe: heat. Constant winds parched the Warmside's lakes and rivers. Grasses and flowers withered, and trees sickened. Dust devils danced across the desiccated plain. Because the rock giant was partly flesh, his soft parts succumbed to the heat. He collapsed under a rocky overhang that lay at the base of a needlerock. By the next Moon-Rising, he no longer moved. I learned all this much later from my sprite friends, the Loblin, who saw vultures circling over his fallen body. His stony hide may have protected him, but I doubt it.

"I did not share my friends' fate. I left the island. In one sack, I carried a vellum-paged book, bound in stiff leather, a grimoire I'd found hiding within a stone wall of the tower standing on the island in the Coldside Sea. Conjurations filled its pages. In that codex of magic, I found enchantments I used to call on the Great Forces when I needed their help.

"I reached the Coldside shore by using a spell from that book." Rocánonom's finger traced the route from the island tower to the shore of Dragonwolder's Coldside.

"I feared I'd drown in the sea storm raging between the island and the Coldside. I searched the grimoire and found a spell to calm the surface of the sea. I sailed across its glossy expanse to safety.

"After hiding my boat on the beach, I trekked through a river valley and mountain passes until I reached the low rolling hills and meadows that would become known as Anonom Trace. The mountains I crossed might have crushed me with falling rocks, but at my utterance of another spell, gusts of wind pushed me gently up the slopes and righted me whenever I stumbled. As I traveled, I learned many powerful incantations drawing forth the Great Forces. Never had I been so close to the Ways of the World.

"I rested in the Trace and waited for the other giants but, well, I've told you what happened to them."

Alana's hand brushed the other scrolls, still tightly bound with cord. "Are these pages of your grim—grim—how do you say it?"

"No, not at all. The grimoire is a book I hid after studying it a bit more. Only the one who possesses it may summon the Great Forces. It should be safe now.

"When I was studying the grimoire, I learned secrets belonging to the Ways of the World. Remember how the ice dome and fog over the lodge protected you from the aiglonax when you were a child?"

"How could I forget? You chanted some old song, and a sheet of solid ice curved over us. The beast screamed with rage. He couldn't break through it."

"Not 'some old song,' Alana, but an incantation calling upon wind, water, and earth Elementals. They looked like dragon spirits. I learned how to harness the power of dragon Elementals. Without that power, I never could have fought the Malevir. Not long after I settled in the Anonom Trace, the book's enchantments also helped me free the Loblin from their underground hideouts."

"The Loblin lived underground? How? They're not much taller than my knee."

"Yes, like their ancestors the UrLoblin, they once lived on mountain slopes and in rock shelters that faced the Coldside Desert, but basilisks and other beasts attacked them time and again. The little ones fled into the Veiled Valley's red clay underearth. That's when the Loblin or their ancestors dug nearly every tunnel running under the valley and through the mountains."

"Now I understand how they led us so easily through all those tunnels and passageways when the Malevir was attacking us. But that grim—grimoire—who worked its magic before you found it?"

"The book is from another time, when World-Turns were shorter, and the sun was hotter than it is today. The Malevir found it on the island and used it for as many World-Turns as there are trees on this hill—but I didn't exactly *find* it. I freed it from the Malevir. Now he wants it back."

"So, he turned into a dragonrider, a hork, then the aiglonax—all to find you and take back the grimoire?"

"Could be. I don't know what the Malevir is now. If Kurnan truly hears voices, then I fear they belong to the Malevir. He's using your brother to repossess that magick."

Alana gripped the table, nearly spilling her cider across the scrolls. "The Malevir? You say the beast controls my brother?"

The giant stepped away from the table and poured the rest of his cider into the hearth. "I think, through Kurnan, the Malevir aims to take back the grimoire's powers. If he does, he will attack the very Ways of the World and rip away all strength, wit, and magical powers from our dragon friends."

AURYKK

WAKING IN THE BACK room of his lair, the warmest spot in his network of tunnels and chambers, the Golden Dragon Aurykk raised his head. He yawned and stretched his hind legs then twisted his neck to inspect new patches of dusty white scales on his side. Even after living for more than four hundred World-Turns, Aurykk was surprised to see those dull patches, sure signs of coming into his Twilight Time. Although he yearned for long naps and easy food, he refused to retire from his work as a Protector. He was ready to help if called.

Aurykk licked his fangs and his belly growled. A snack would be good. He nosed through clusters of gems scattered about his nest until he found a few black pearls, his favorites. He opened his huge jaws and, with his long, muscular tongue, flicked three pearls into his mouth. In mid-swallow, he paused. A shadow passed the window in the room's outer wall then flitted by again. Aurykk stood with effort and lumbered closer to his observatory. He coughed out one of the pearls. "Visitors?" He sighed. "Of course. I should have expected them."

Aurykk sniffed the floor around his feet until he found the pearl. He flipped it into his mouth, rolled it around his tongue, and grunted as he swallowed the smooth, dark treat. On heavy feet, he passed through a long gallery decorated with scenes of dragons overpowering monsters. At the end of the gallery, Aurykk stretched his neck into another chamber of the Orferans' Cave of Refuge. He squinted against the dazzling light that flooded the chamber through the cave's opening. Seeing no intruders, Aurykk grunted again then filled a pot with fresh water, which he placed on a high stone platform in the middle of the chamber. He blasted the platform with his fiery breath until it glowed purple-red. The water began to boil. Into the pot he tossed herbs, including crimpfever and fenugreek. Then he breathed in their warm fragrance and closed his eyes.

"May we come in?"

His nephew's voice broke into Aurykk's reverie, and he blinked. A dragon silhouette stood framed by the cave's entrance and the sunlit world behind it. "Yes, Draako, please come in. I was expecting you." He settled back on his haunches, and curls of sweet white smoke rose from his nostrils toward the cave ceiling. "I knew that you were anxious to see me."

Draako showed his surprise by belching a few cinders, but he quickly steadied himself and urged his rider to enter the cave. "Come in, Nnylf. You know you are welcome. Uncle, how did you guess?"

"Guess?" Aurykk snorted. "Nonsense. I do not guess. Join me now around the hearth. Let's share some tea and talk."

Draako sat by his side and deeply inhaled the herbal steam hanging over the heated platform. Nnylf found a seat carved into a concave rock opposite the dragons. Extending his forepaws, Aurykk offered him a jar of warm tea and then, as relaxed as a huge cat remembering a succulent mouse snack, he lowered himself to the floor.

Draako began, "Uncle, you look well. How have you been?"

"I *am* well, Draako. I have been resting—until lately. Something has changed, maybe for the worse. I think we are sensing the Malevir's presence again, aren't we?"

Nnylf placed his jar on the floor and walked around the platform until he was close to Aurykk's snout. "Does he want to find a way to attack us again?"

"How could he do that without his aiglonax, Aindle?"

"Please don't tease me. You once used all your strength to revive dragon ancestor spirits, unite them with the valley folk, and lead our attack on the aiglonax." He looked at Draako for support. "Didn't we destroy the Malevir that day?"

Draako picked at a small rodent bone caught behind his fang. "After our victory, we were sure the Veiled Valley was rid of the Malevir's attacks, yet I fear the beast is with us again. Look at what happened in Fossarelick."

"Tell me more," said Aurykk.

Draako continued. "People, even his own sister, say that Kurnan acts like one possessed by the beast's dark spirit. They think he took that amulet Nnylf found in Aindle's ashes and fled Fossarelick with it."

Nnylf asked, "Why is Kurnan acting this way? He should have recovered by now, like Sweetnettle. The aiglonax poisoned our Lobli friend twice, but *he* recovered."

"The Lobli has a belly heart *and* a shoulder heart—two hearts heal faster than Kurnan's one and only. Remember too, rue broth defended Sweetnettle against the beast, but Kurnan had none before he was poisoned."

Nnylf paced around Aurykk's hearth. He tore his cap from his head and ran his fingers through his thick curls. "But I saw the aiglonax crumble to dust."

Aurykk belched a puff of cinders. "Aindle the aiglonax died, but not the Malevir. The beast found a new tool in Kurnan. Somehow, he helped Kurnan steal the amulet. He then lured him away from your village, Nnylf. Where is Kurnan now? Have you seen him?"

"Yes, and he seems lost or confused," said Nnylf. "We thought he was heading toward the Coldside Sea, but he turned toward the Warmside instead. Very odd. What does he think he will find there?"

"I'm sure Kurnan doesn't know. He has no idea. The Malevir is pushing him, forcing him somehow, and probably toward something that will further his terrible purpose."

Draako stood in front of Aurykk. "Through that amulet!" He tapped his uncle's snout with his own. "I am pleased you are well. Your advice helped us think clearly about this. We'll follow Kurnan now and stop him before he harms himself."

"And the Veiled Valley," muttered Nnylf.

"Yes, the valley." Draako nodded. "I regret to say we must leave you but thank you."

Aurykk stood and looked into Draako's amber eyes. "Are you going to the Warmside, then?"

"Yes, as you suggested."

"Oh, did I? Good! You will find help when you reach the Warmside. Seek out the rock giant, Enderfon. You will find him near a towering red needlerock. Follow the dry river bed crossing the land."

"Not Enderfon, surely? They say he died out there, long ago."

"So *they* say." Aurykk ambled with Draako and Nnylf to the terrace outside the cave. "You will hear Enderfon's story in the Warmside, I assure you." Wishing them a safe flight, he trudged back into the cave's dark interior.

Sitting back on his haunches by the observatory window, Aurykk watched heavy, dark clouds settle over the mountaintops. In a short time, he could see nothing more than roiling mists past his window. He shivered; the whiskers around his snout twitched as he sought a certain smell in the humid air. "Soon, soon, we will meet again." Aurykk sighed and scratched a patch of itchy scales with his hind leg.

SWEETNETTLE

LAYERS OF PLUSH REEDCLOTH wrapped his soft copper-colored boots, but Sweetnettle shivered as he waded through the last snowfield. He strained against cold, battering winds to reach the Warmside outlands before dark. His strength was holding up, but this task was no fun. He mused on the way he had regained his strength after Aindle's attacks. Few beings had survived a basilisk's poison, but infusions of rue broth and other herbal brews had revived him. Sweetnettle patted his comforting round belly as he remembered the broth's taste—burnt bread crust and vinegar, sweetened with root sugar.

Rocánonom's words echoed in Sweetnettle's head. *My friend, your news from Fossarelick worries me. The Malevir's strength grows again. Go to the Warmside, where the great Enderfon lies. You'll find him by a red needlerock. Close to whatever is left of the giant should be his mace, Rowel. Use it.*

Duty pushed him forward. He closed his mind to all other thoughts until, sensing his feet no longer struggling in deep snow, he looked back at the land he had crossed. The snowfield, with its steaming ice and glassy surface, was behind him. He had entered the Warmside.

Sweetnettle chewed his lower lip and said to himself, "I hate this place, where we Loblin spent long, sad days underground, far from the sun." He sighed. "Rocánonom, if only you could hear me. You said I must go where Enderfon died. You said I must poke around his skeleton by the red needlerock. Well then, this Lobli—me—says I will eat first to keep up my strength." Sweetnettle scanned the area but saw only one spot that looked inviting enough for a picnic. He adjusted his sack's shoulder strap and headed toward a broad hillock.

When he reached the side of the rise facing away from the sun, Sweetnettle tugged at a small red cloth in his sack, flipped it open in the breeze, and spread it on the shaded, spongey ground. He wriggled his bottom until it settled comfortably into a hollow. Humming a little five-note tune, he snatched at a fruit and nut bun floating out of his open sack. A second bun and a pod of nectar followed.

Sweetnettle plucked his treats out of the air. He nibbled, then gulped, until they disappeared. After burping quietly and patting his belly, he stood up, shook some crumbs off the cloth, and tucked it into his sack. In a few short bounds, he reached the top of the hillock and looked all around for the site of Enderfon's remains.

With the Veiled Valley behind him, he studied the warmside horizon. In the distance, he saw the outline of a long, high ridge, an escarpment. It sat behind rolling slopes striped by lines of scree and rockfall. At its highest point stood the towering red needlerock, casting its shadow across a wide, nearly dry river bed.

Certain he'd find Enderfon's remains, Sweetnettle tucked his boot wrappings into his sack, sitting snuggly on his hip, and set off to complete his task. Although he was enjoying the sun's warmth and the absence of this Cold-Turn's bitter chill, the growing Warmside heat began to weigh him down.

"Perhaps I *should* find an old Loblin tunnel," he muttered. "What with the hot sun and mud caking my boots, I would be cooler and cleaner underground—but, no." He shook his head. "It's dark down there and I'd be so alone." He shivered at the memory of forced marches and the cold, dank passageways that he and his fellow sprites had dug long ago to escape predators. The memories quickened his footsteps.

Scattered stubbly trees clung to the soft earth with a lattice of exposed roots. His toe slipped under one root elbowing out of the muck, and he tripped. With his hands splayed out behind him, he sat and looked around. Cool sawgrass with its serrated edges tickled his palms. His eyelids grew heavy and his legs began to ache.

Sweetnettle was about to lie back for a little nap when he noticed his hands sinking into the soggy earth. "Ways of the World! I'm sitting on Somnifer Grass! If I'd fallen asleep, it would have eaten me." Groaning, he pulled himself to his feet, wiped his hands with his red rag, and brushed little chunks of mud from the seat of his leggings. His feet would sink into the muck unless he found some way to travel through it more lightly.

"Rocánonom, what shall I do?" he called to the breezes that blew from the sunsetside. As if answering him, a memory of a long-passed conversation with the giant made him smile. *Before Aindle's spell changed your kind into goblins, you had wings. Did you forget how to fly?* Sweetnettle's belly heart fluttered at the memory and a pain he wanted to forget.

He rubbed the sides of his neck then fingered two thin, bony ridges that ran from the corners of his jaw to right above his shoulder blades. With a sigh of resignation, he squeezed his eyes shut until tiny colored dots danced behind his eyelids as he uttered:

Spend the wind and spare no pain.
Flutter fast like falling rain.
Let me reach the sky again.
Wings! Sprout!

Sweetnettle howled. His neck ridges thickened and began to push through his skin. He knelt and thrust his palms into the soft earth. With handfuls of dirt oozing from his clenched fists, he fainted face-down among blades of soothing sawgrass.

When he next opened his eyes, his pain was dulling, but grass and mud were swallowing him. He pushed himself up. Although mud splotched his tunic and leggings, he worried more about his gear than his clothing. Reaching for his sack he touched the soft membrane of a wing. Turning his head to see the results of his summoning song, he smiled. Two nearly transparent gossamer wings opened and closed behind him as he knit his brow and worked his shoulder muscles.

"When my skin closes and the wings stretch fully, I will test them." The grasslands spread out before him. He turned to face the escarpment and relished the silence that lay over the land.

But not for long. A scream pierced the silence, and Sweetnettle shuddered as shouts and groans followed. He heard footsteps steadily approaching through the muck. Sweetnettle ducked into a thick clump of sawgrass and covered his nose with a rag. *Can't fall asleep now.* He yanked his cap from his head, folded his new wings, and hoped that his green speckled skin and brown curls would hide him from the intruder. Sawgrass scratching his cheeks, he peered over waving sedge leaves and gasped as a young man passed only a few body lengths from him.

The fellow was shrieking a stream of curses, apparently to himself for no one was with him. Wearing ragged Cold-Turn wraps and leggings, he lugged a bulging sack on his back. The young man trudged toward the escarpment, and Sweetnettle crouched lower in the sawgrass.

The Lobli's two hearts beat quickly in unison. *Kurnan! Here? Why?* He crept through the tall sedge and followed in Kurnan's path.

❧

Shadows cast by the massive escarpment hid Sweetnettle as he watched Kurnan climb scree-covered slopes leading to the needlerock. The young man reached a shallow ledge, threw down his sack, and looked in every direction. Seemingly satisfied he was alone, Kurnan rested against the slope.

Sweetnettle twitched his little pointed ears to catch Kurnan's words. He flinched as Kurnan tugged his own hair and wailed, "Leave me alone. You promised me peace. You broke your promise. I want to go back."

Sweetnettle looked for the object of Kurnan's outburst, but the man was still alone. After one last echoing cry, Kurnan lay facedown on the ledge and, with a long, low moan, he pulled his knees to his chest. The sprite ignored his natural urge to ease the young man's woes with his sack of remedies, for who knew what terrible wraiths possessed him? Best to lie low and watch. Or better yet, while Kurnan lay with his head tucked into his chest, he'd fly to a higher hiding place.

The escarpment cast long shadows and gave Sweetnettle relief from the rising heat of the sawgrass marsh as he flew up. Weariness enveloped him, and soon he was asleep on top of a rock tucked into the slope. He had no idea how long he had been asleep when Kurnan's piercing cry had awakened him.

"What mace? Leave me be!" Kurnan shouted. He crouched, leaped off the ledge, and landed near a wide fan of scree at the base. He lay there, in the grass, without moving.

Sweetnettle flew down, tucked in his wings, and dashed through rows of sedge, mindless of rough thickets and sharp blades of grass that grasped at his sleeves and leggings. Reaching Kurnan's side, Sweetnettle used his knee to raise the unconscious young man's head. He wiped a bleeding cut on Kurnan's cheek with a corner of his red rag then dipped his three fingers into a clay jar of pink salve and dabbed the wound. The bleeding stopped, and the cut began to close. Sweetnettle wrapped Kurnan's senseless fingers around two nectar pods, listened to the young man's heartbeat and, satisfied that he was alive with no other injuries, he kicked him awake then turned back to the escarpment and his rock.

Mists from the marshland continued to rise as dusk approached, making it difficult to climb the rocky slope. His persistent fingers poked into a notch here and a hole there until he reached a slab in the talus at the foot of the needlerock. From there, he looked down to the dimming marsh and saw Kurnan drain his nectar pods and stumble coldside, away from the escarpment. Heading back to the Cold-Turn snowfields, Kurnan swatted the air behind him as if deflecting a swarm of biting insects, all the while screaming insults to the air.

Assured that Kurnan no longer showed interest in climbing the escarpment, Sweetnettle relaxed and set up his camp for the night. The sky toward Sunsetside was still light, but he knew that darkness would come quickly and he wasted no time building a little hut. He held out his hand and hummed a new five-note tune, and a small flame danced on his palm. He tossed the flame onto a pile of dried grass, herbs, and stalks. Fragrant clumps of fraxinella ignited, and the kindling flared up. As Sweetnettle wriggled within the warmth of his shelter, he watched the little hearth's blue flames dance in the dark. His heavy eyelids drooped, and sleep enfolded him once more.

With the morning's first light, Sweetnettle was well on his way to the other side of the needlerock. He braced himself for the sight of gigantic bleached bones. He expected to find them in a cluttered pile around a mace ten times larger than a sprite. "I'll need one of Rocánonom's spells to move that thingummy from here, I'm sure."

As Sweetnettle grasped a jutting rock edge to pull himself around a corner, he heard a low, rolling rumble. Instinctively, he looked at the top of the needlerock, but nothing was swaying. He laid his small palm on the rockwall. No quaking. He paused and listened. The air was still.

His tight shoulders relaxed. At that moment, a booming roll of thunder crashed above him, but no storm clouds were overhead. Holding his breath, he raised one tiny foot. He planted his toes, then his heel, now the second foot—toes down, then heel—across the gravel-strewn rock floor. He repeated the careful movement a few more times until he reached the far side of the needlerock. The ground shook, and an immense shadow cast darkness around him. He darted behind the rock wall and tried to catch his breath. His hearts were fluttering again. "Calm, calm. None of that now, hearts. Slow down. Whatever it is, it won't notice me."

Sweetnettle peeked around the corner. Sitting on the edge of the plateau, facing the Low Beyond, was a mass of rock in the shape of a man more than twice the size of Rocánonom. His legs, thick as tree trunks, dangled over the edge of the plateau. His hefty sky-blue arms hung at his sides. The giant grunted, and his hands cracked open, the sound echoing as he reached overhead and stretched. Lowering his arms, the giant sat back, lifted his jutting chin, and began to sing.

> Falling, falling. Was I asleep?
> I heard my brother's call today.
> Within my heart, it lay so deep.
> It chased my aching dreams away.
> In Dragonwolder, no more to weep,
> I'll rise to find the hero's way.

The giant's voice was soft and sweet, like waves lapping the seashore during a Warm-Turn. Hoping that the giant would be as gentle a friend as Rocánonom, Sweetnettle crept out of his shadow and cleared his throat. "Oh, sir, if you are not a wraith, a ghost, or an apparition of the great Enderfon, please look with kindness upon me, this little Lobli called Sweetnettle, for I mean you no harm."

The giant looked down and coughed. A gap-toothed smile softened his knobby cheeks as he croaked, "A Lobli? From the Veiled Valley may I hope?"

"Yes, sent by your friend Rocánonom, alive these many World-Turns. He—we both—thought the Warmside killed you. I expected to find a heap of bones here."

"The Malevir's enchantment nearly did finish me and turn my fleshy parts to stone, but the sun's heat wrapped me in deep sleep until a call woke me. Must have been Rocánonom's, for you say he lives and sent you."

Sweetnettle's hurried answer sent words tumbling over each other. "Yes, he sent me because signs of the Malevir are popping up all over Dragonwolder. To fight him, Rocánonom sent me to find your mace...oh, sorry, I meant to say your amazing self. What might I do for you? Do you feel pain? I'm a Lobli and I help those in need, be they humans, giants, dragons, or creatures of the wild. Do you still have your mace? Oops." The sprite grimaced and hung his head.

"Ah, my mace. Yes, I am happy to say that I still have it." Enderfon laughed and his neck creaked as he turned. Bits of rock broke off and slid down his back. He knelt beside Sweetnettle. One hand rested on his jagged knee while the other stretched toward the rock wall. "Look, little friend of giants. This one here—I call her Rowel."

A long shaft was leaning against the wall where, moments before, Sweetnettle had seen only a mass of rock. Green and white gems studded each spike of its heavy head; they sparkled in the morning's sunlight. Enderfon grasped the shaft with one hand and raised the mace high over his head.

Sweetnettle fled around the rockwall corner as Enderfon slammed the mace into the plateau's floor. The gems emitted widening soft circles of green and white light. Every patch of gravel-strewn ground touched by the light turned into moist brown soil. Within a few moments, little green sprouts poked through the earth and uncurled toward the sun. Sweetnettle remembered hearing about another light like that, hidden deep in the dragons' ancestral lair.

"My arm's awake now, it is." Enderfon laid the shaft on the ground and rubbed his slab of a shoulder. "How many World-Turns did I miss while I napped?"

"Too many."

Enderfon rubbed his belly and the sound of clattering stones knocked against Sweetnettle's ears. "I am a bit hungry," said the giant. "Do you carry food in that sack of yours?"

"Yes, mere Loblin morsels. We'll need a chant stronger than any of mine to conjure up fare for a giant's appetite."

Enderfon smiled and his alabaster teeth gleamed. "I have just the chant we'll need to make a feast for both of us."

Sweetnettle sat cross-legged on the plateau floor, now covered with soft, pale green grass. His pointed ears twitched as Enderfon hummed a tune based on eight rising and falling notes. The sound was so deep in the giant's throat that Sweetnettle imagined the air itself was thrumming and dancing around them. He pulled his pulsing sack off his shoulder and laid it on the grass between him and the giant.

The sack bulged and twisted. Its flap snapped open, and Enderfon had Sweetnettle reach inside. He pulled out a flat brown disk.

"Put the disk on the grass next to the sack, if you will. Now, do you have some water we could sprinkle on it?" Enderfon asked.

Sweetnettle sprinkled droplets of water from his gourd across the top of the disk. As soon as the droplets pooled on its surface, the disk plumped up. The disk became a savory pie, bigger than the giant's hand. The pie's delicious aroma reminded the sprite of roasted mushrooms and nuts, of cheeses and berries and, most of all, the honey-laced cakes he loved so much. "Tell me, what you have made for us, Enderfon?"

"Ah, the food I liked most when I went trekking—roasted granite and savory pebbles. You must share with me."

"Loblin don't eat granite, kind giant. Anyway, that pie doesn't look like roasted rock."

"Your piece will taste like mushrooms, nuts, berries, and bits of cake. May I offer you some?"

With a trill of giggles, Sweetnettle held out his hand. Enderfon cut a small slice and pressed it into his palm. It tasted as it smelled— delicious and warm. Enderfon tore large chunks from the pie and licked his lips after every swallow. Soon they had eaten their fill. They wiped their mouths and rested against the rockwall, Sweetnettle sitting close to the giant's thigh.

"Are you ready to travel coldside with me?" Enderfon asked.

"But aren't we going to bring the mace to Rocánonom?"

"Ah, no. We are going to follow that young man—what is his name?"

"Kurnan. But how did you know—"

"I, too, sensed the Malevir's presence when Kurnan climbed the slope."

"Kurnan stole the Malevir's amulet."

"Ah, then I did sense the beast's power as my eyes began to open. Lobli, we must destroy the amulet. My mace will help. It holds awesome magick."

"Magick powerful enough to fight the Malevir?"

"In some ways. It could kill a dragon or bring it back to life. Now, Sweetnettle of the Veiled Valley, you say I missed too many World-Turns during my sleep. Why?"

"Because you missed how Rocánonom and the Orferans helped people settle in the Veiled Valley. When the Malevir attacked them again and again, they could have used your help."

"Who were the Orferans?"

"A dragon clan and the valley's Protectors, led by Aurykk the Golden."

"Dragons. They came back?"

"More than anyone would have expected. They defended the valley with their strength and magick. Rocánonom used his powers, too."

"How strong *are* his powers?"

Sweetnettle shrugged. "I do know he cannot fight the Malevir by himself."

"Why did he not come here with you?"

"From his tower by the Coldside Sea, he has been watching for signs of the Malevir. Seeing the signs, he sent me to find…to find…"

"To find a weapon. My mace or, better yet, myself. We must tell him about Kurnan and about me."

Sweetnettle gulped, and his belly heart thumped a little. "I'd better send him a message right now. Perhaps I must go back or…look!"

A small flock of chary birds was roosting on the branches of a tree growing out of the rockwall near them. The birds were eyeing Enderfon's pie and looking sadly at crumbs scattered across the patch of grass. They chirped and hopped then fluttered down to the lowest branch near the giant and cocked their heads as Sweetnettle pursed his lips and whistled.

"I'm calling to you, chary birds," Sweetnettle sang out. "Who is the bravest among you? Who dares to come close to us and eat these lovely crumbs? You could be my messenger to the great giant Rocánonom. He will feed you warm porridge and crisp seeds when you bring him my message." One of the little green and blue birds flew to the grass and began to peck at the bits of pie. Others followed, and all of them ate until not one crumb remained.

The birds nestled into the grass while Sweetnettle wrote his note on a scrap of bark paper. "Which of you has enough strength to carry this message to Rocánonom's tower by the Coldside Sea?"

The plump leader of the flock stood up and puffed out the ruff under his beak, but a much smaller and not as brightly hued bird landed on Enderfon's toe. She raised a wing to volunteer.

She bobbed her little head when Sweetnettle asked her if she was ready. He sealed his message and tied it to the bird's leg. Enderfon gently tossed the chary bird into the air, and she flew away toward the Sunsetside Mountains and the Coldside Sea. The rest of the flock followed.

"There goes a brave little one," whispered Enderfon. "Now, come closer. We must make plans."

Sweetnettle unfurled his small, silky wings and landed on the giant's shoulder. "Yes, and quickly before the Malevir's strength grows within the boy."

NNYLF

THEIR FLIGHT FROM THE Cave of Refuge down to the grasslands of the Warmside began over snow-covered fields surrounding
Fossarelick. Nnylf wondered if healthy new barley shoots would break
through the now-frozen soil once the Cold-Turn left the land. Dull and
gray under the short day's pale light, the fields did not look promising.
Icy winds swept around him and Nnylf shivered. His hands were numb
and, more than once, he nearly lost his grip on Draako's neck frill.

*Careful, my rider. I don't want to lose you. Wrap your left hand in
the end of your sleeve and reach toward my jaw.*

Nnylf leaned forward until he lay over the frill. His head rested
on the bony ridge behind his dragon's ear. His arm, stretched to its
limit, nearly popped out of its socket. Draako's tongue thrust a small
steaming packet into Nnylf's open palm.

*Quickly, now. Tuck the cinder packet between your armor and
your tunic. That should warm you up.*

A deep, comforting warmth spread across Nnylf's belly and
encircled his waist. He heard Draako's voice. *Once we reach the
Warmside, you won't need it for the sun will warm us again. We shall
find Kurnan and reclaim the amulet.*

With a wistful smile, Nnylf nodded. His head ached as memories of Kurnan as a little boy flashed in his thoughts: his sweet nature, his courage as a dragonrider, and his nearly being killed by the aiglonax. Finding Kurnan should be easy; they would catch him in his wanderings across the Veiled Valley and into the Warmside. But could they make him give up the amulet and come home? Kurnan, grumpy and unpredictable, feared no dragon and certainly no one from Fossarelick.

The sky cleared. Nnylf's dragon friend soared over forests that bordered the Protectors' Lodge toward the Warmside. Buffeting winds became gentle breezes. The smell of wet earth and rotting plants wafted through the air. Nnylf lifted his sweating head from Draako's comforting, solid neck and looked down. A rough boundary line of melting ice marked the beginning of marshy Warmside lands. He searched for Kurnan, but nothing moved, neither through the thick grasses below them nor over the snow behind them.

Without warning, a bevy of chary birds flew up and around the dragon's head. Nnylf ducked his head for a moment as they darted at him; then he stretched out an arm to snatch at one of the birds swooping past him. His hand closed around a little one. He gripped Draako tightly with his knees as a tiny pale blue and green bird trembled in the tight cup of his palms. Nnylf spoke softly to it and stroked its head. "What is this, little one? A note, tied to your leg? Is it for me?"

The bird shook violently, and Nnylf feared it would die. He released it and sent his thoughts to Draako. *What do they want of us? Can you speak to them, my friend? Can you hear their thoughts?*

Draako did not answer, but he flew closer to the earth and two other birds landed on the dragon's long snout. The fatter one fluffed his brilliant green and blue feathers and chirped a stream of notes from his upraised beak.

He says that a giant and a Lobli sent them Sunsetside to find Rocánonom. They have a message for him. They said we could find the giant by a red needlerock.

Could it be the giant Enderfon, just as Aurykk said? I'm glad I left the note tied to the little bird's leg.

You did well. Look, I see the needlerock. Hold on, I'm going to turn sharply.

Nnylf hunkered down and lowered his head again into Draako's frill. The dragon moved his neck and tail like a fish as he changed direction and headed toward the needlerock. Draako then dived sideways, slowly for Nnylf's sake. Gaining lift from the breezes, he leveled off, spread his wings, and coasted until they were close to the escarpment. Something stirred on a broad ledge partway up the cliff. It was very big.

ISABELLA

BEFORE SUNRISING, ORANGE LIGHT flowed out of the rock shelter's low-slung arched entrance. Curled in the shelter's deepest recess, Isabella warmed its rock floor with a steady low flame. After dampening her smoke glands, she patted the floor—*warm enough for my rider.* She burst into a loud, roaring dragon song. Soon, Alana and Rocánonom came running. The girl, in her tunic and armor, dashed into the grotto and began stroking Isabella's lowered snout.

The giant dallied at the entrance, pressed his knuckles into his hips, and grinned. "I'm glad to see you defended us from all those fiendish attackers, my lady Isabella."

"Attackers? What attackers?" Alana choked on her surprise and bent forward to catch her breath.

Rocánonom strode to her side. "Your dragon friend thought it was time for us to leave our warm beds and join her for breakfast. See how she has warmed the rock shelter for us? Stay here, Alana. I'll bring some porridge and a few tasty bits for Isabella's morning meal too."

"No need, friend," Isabella said. "I have that morsel, over there." She pointed to the huge frozen green snake sticking out of a snowdrift. "A delicious way to start my day."

Alana shivered and sank to the heated floor. Rocánonom promised to return with breakfast and her cloak. Then he waved and made his way back to the tower.

Daylight grew stronger, and breaks appeared in the ever-present clouds. Isabella scanned the sky. *This cold World-Turn is in its last Moon-Risings. Too soon the icy winds will die. Too soon, if we ever hope to stop Kurnan.*

Isabella stood. A wave of sadness flowed through her at the memory of her erstwhile rider. Sickened by the aiglonax's poison, Kurnan had lost his sweetness and his yen for dragonriding. Her little bird, felled by a monstrous beast of prey. Isabella was startled by Alana's coughing. Her sighs had wrapped the young woman's head in smoke.

Isabella flinched. The sound of fluttering bird wings turned her attention to the shelter's entrance. She heard the tower door slam. *Rocánonom is standing at its threshold.*

"Something odd is happening. Come, Alana. Let's see what has kept Rocánonom from bringing your porridge."

The girl rose to her feet with a little whimper. "Very well. I am cold and half-starved, if you must know." She followed Isabella out of the rock shelter and up the slope.

Isabella swept her rider into the folds of a wing and bounded up the slope. Once she landed on the terrace of Rocánonom's tower, she let Alana press into her side to stay warm. The girl peered over the wing's bony membrane. A cloud of chary birds was circling the giant's head. Rocánonom extended one long arm, and the smallest of the birds, with a dull green throat and blue wing feathers, perched on his wrist.

A piece of bark was tied to one of its legs. "I think that bird is asking us to unwrap the bark paper and read it," Isabella said. "Alana, distract the other birds. Fetch a handful of grain from Rocánonom's stores and scatter some at his feet."

Isabella opened her wing and Alana ran inside the tower. Soon she returned, draped in her cloak. She held a half-eaten barley bun in one hand and, in the other, she clutched some dried barley stalks. All the birds except the one clinging to Rocánonom's wrist flew to meet her. Alana scattered the stalks on the ground at the giant's feet. Hungry after their long flight, every bird but the messenger swooped and pecked at seeds.

Rocánonom stroked the littlest chary bird's head while Alana offered it a tiny piece of her bun. After lifting its beak as it swallowed the morsel, the bird trilled a high-pitched tune and offered its leg bearing the bark paper. Alana untied the string and, pinching the paper between her thumb and forefinger, she slid it off the bird's slender leg and unrolled the message.

"Shall I read it to you?" she asked. "It's so tiny, barely the size of your thumb."

Rocánonom nodded while Isabella blinked and thought, *I know what it says.*

"Well then, it's signed 'Sweetnettle, your friend,' and it says that he's with a rock giant, Enderfon. They will leave the needlerock and track Kurnan, who is heading to the Coldside."

The giant took a few moments to lower the messenger into the flock of feasting chary birds, then he stood and asked to see the message. His thick fingers fumbled with it, and he returned it to Alana. "Please read it to us again. Indeed, my hands are too big to hold it, and they're shaking."

Isabella's heart leaped. *Another legendary giant is alive.* She watched as Alana read the message and Rocánonom raked his fingers through his red curls. *Why is he so upset? He should be celebrating.*

"My friends, I thought my brother giant Enderfon died long ago. I sent Sweetnettle warmside to a red needlerock and hoped he would retrieve Enderfon's mace, but Enderfon lives. I don't understand."

Isabella asked, "Why did you want the mace?"

"If Enderfon had reached the Veiled Valley at the same time I did, he would have used the mace to ready the land for planting." Rocánonom paused and cleared his throat. "The mace's magick is great."

Alana swallowed the last of her barley bun. "But with the next Warm-Turn, valley folk will have no need of it."

"Not to plant, but to defend us and the Scintilla. Even now, the Malevir uses the amulet, luring Kurnan toward the Coldside Mountains into dangerous and uncharted places."

"We dragons know those places well," Isabella said in a low growl. "My mother, Serpinafria, died on those mountains. Can't we keep Kurnan from going there?"

"Not yet. The Malevir controls him. I do not know the reason, but I can guess. The amulet contains a piece of the Malevir's powers. If the beast takes it back, he will be more powerful than ever."

Alana swiped crumbs from her lips with the back of her hand. "Rocánonom, how would the mace help us?"

"It could weaken the powers locked in the amulet. Enderfon knows the dangers your brother faces while under the Malevir's spell. His mace might keep the amulet away from the Malevir. Now, let us think about what we can do to stop Kurnan."

Isabella stretched her enormous copper wings. They cast a shadow over the startled birds and her companions. "Alana, our giant friend is right. We should go now. We must find Kurnan before he reaches the mountains."

Rocánonom shook his head. "Isabella, remember, while he wears the amulet, Kurnan will resist you and even his sister. Call Nnylf and Draako. Fly to the needlerock with them and join Enderfon. Above all, keep yourselves safe."

Isabella listened to her rider's jumbled thoughts; in the young woman's heart, deep sadness for her brother struggled with anger and fear of the Malevir. *I hear you, Alana. Soon we shall meet Draako. I am sending my thoughts.*

Alana squatted next to the flock of birds and offered a finger to the little messenger. After bobbing several times, the bird hopped onto her finger, which Alana brought close to her face. "Our small friend, you are a fine messenger. Will you fly with us now and help us protect my little brother?"

The little bird ruffled her neck feathers then flew down to the ground and hopped over to her flock's leader. They exchanged chirps and trills, while bobbing their heads several times, until the little one apparently had permission to join Alana and Isabella's mission.

Isabella opened her jaws. *Hop in, tiny friend. No, I shall not eat you. A crispy giant scorpion would be more to my liking. Make yourself cozy in my warm jaw pouch, stocked with seeds. I will carry you safely over the cold land.*

Alana fetched her belongings from inside the tower and, wrapped tightly in her cloak, she climbed up her dragon's extended leg until Isabella could feel the young woman settling onto her neck hump. With a deep bow of farewell to Rocánonom, Isabella crouched then sprang into icy Cold-Turn winds. She circled the hilltop once and nodded as Rocánonom waved his cap in farewell.

KURNAN

HIS LEGS ACHED, BUT Kurnan's feet danced across the glazed expanse of snow. Muddy muck no longer tugged at his feet. The voices stopped pounding against the inside of his forehead. Only twice, as he pushed onward, did he hear their whispers: "Follow that frozen streambed" or "Turn there, at that rotted tree." His body followed their bidding, with stops for bites of stale bread crusts or a sip from that strange little pod. *Why should I care where the voices take me? They said this amulet will free me. They must know. It doesn't matter anymore.* He broke the frozen surface of a pond with a few sharp kicks of his boot heel. Kneeling, he filled his gourd and gulped the glacial water.

After sealing and stowing his gourd, Kurnan looked into the distance ahead. As usual, the valley was living up to its name. Even during this Winter-Turn, ground mist shrouded the land. Beyond, the dark silhouette of the Coldside Mountains loomed against a dull gray sky.

Kurnan turned toward the pond again. The boom of breaking ice caught his ear. Cracks zigzagged across the pond's surface. Slabs of ice tilted on end then thudded into each other and sank under sloshing waves. He gaped at a glistening mound of water rising from the middle of the pond, like a giant bubble in a boiling pot. As the bubble burst, a dark mass surged out of it.

The amulet, a voice called. *Squeeze it. Repeat this chant: Sreturpu uprooters. Ta-erter. Thus, the Rivelam.*

"What—what are they?" Kurnan could barely speak as he looked at the hunched beasts wading toward him. Covered in long, dripping fur, they raised their arms and glared at him with cavernous red eyes. "Again—tell me the chant again," he gasped.

Say Sreturpu uprooters!

"Sre...sreturpu uprooters!"

Again, Sreturpu uprooters. Ta-erter. Thus, the Rivelam.

"Sreturpu uprooters. Ta-erter. Thus, the Rivelam," Kurnan croaked repeatedly.

The beasts stopped. Steam rose from their stooped bodies, and their low growling rolled like distant thunder. He swallowed the chant when a cloud of freezing pellets wrapped the creatures and they sank into the pond. Kurnan laughed with relief, but only a hoarse cackle left his lips.

Kurnan's raw throat ached. Something was burning his palm and fingers. He let go of the amulet and pressed his hand into the snow until the cold killed his pain. He gripped another handful of snow and wrapped his hand with a rag. "That hurt, you know."

Uprooters hurt more.

Kurnan crouched and tucked the cooling amulet inside his tunic. "What did they want?"

The amulet.

"This?"

Now you see its power. Get up. Go.

"Where to?"

The Coldside Desert.

Kurnan struggled with his sack. "I'm hungry. It hurts." He rubbed his aching ribs.

To the desert. Now.

He looked once more at the pond, but it was calm. Even the spot he had broken at its edge was solid ice. He shivered, tightened his rag bandage, and trudged toward the mountains.

NNYLF

As Draako's flight brought them closer to the red needlerock, Nnylf urged his dragon to fly higher. "I want to look down on the ridge."

At those words, Draako spiraled upward until they were hovering over low-lying clouds hanging above the escarpment. Through a break in the clouds, Nnylf spotted shifting rocks on a cliffside ledge.

"That rockwall's crumbling!" he shouted. "It's a landslide!" A small figure was trapped in the moving mountainside. "And I think a Lobli is caught in it."

That's no landslide. It has a head, arms, and legs.

Nnylf was breathless. "Can't be. The Malevir must have vomited a new monster."

Remember what Aurykk said about Enderfon? Look, the Lobli opened his wings. I'm going to fly closer. Maybe he's in—

"Trouble? Wait," Nnylf interrupted. "I hear Isabella's call."

Me too. She's nearing the Warmside.

Nnylf wished he could soothe his tired thighs, which were pressed into Draako's flanks. "What does she say, Draako? Should we attack that beast?"

No, no—she says the creature is Enderfon. Alana and Isabella bring news from Rocánonom.

∿

Alana was leaning against Isabella's flank while the dragon lounged on her haunches and groomed her tail. Nnylf was sitting near Draako's front leg. Alana's company cheered him but meeting again in this strange place confused him.

He stared at the rock giant, whose body took up half the ledge they occupied. He could not think of anything to say to him or the Lobli, who was perched on the giant's shoulder. Some impulse spurred the sprite to flutter his wings and land next to Alana's right leg. His head reached the young woman's knees.

"Hello, Alana. Do you remember me?"

Nnylf pulled his eyes away from the craggy, towering giant. "How would she know you, Lobli?"

"I do remember him, Nnylf," Alana answered. "You weren't with us, thank the Ways of the World, when the aiglonax attacked Fossarelick folk underground and poisoned this little fellow with the same venom that hurt my brother. After my family rescued him, I helped him recover. Let me introduce you to Sweetnettle, the bravest Lobli of them all."

"Oh, you're *that* Lobli." Nnylf's cheeks pulsed with heat. How could he have forgotten Sweetnettle's kindness? "Of course, I remember you, how you shared nut buns and dried berries with me when we hid from Aindle. I heard about your bravery, how you tried to keep Aindle from the Loblin refuge under the town of Nosidam, how Councilor Prendel became the Malevir's tool despite your biting his leg, how—"

"Stop, stop. Poor Prendel, I wish I could have helped him. Any Lobli would do the same, but Aindle is long gone."

"I'm sorry I didn't recognize you at first. I didn't know you Loblin had wings."

"We sprout wings when we have no choice but to force them. It hurts."

"Oh, Ways of the World, you must be in pain," Nnylf said.

"No, no trouble. I'm fine. But why are *you* all here?"

Nnylf was surprised to hear Isabella answer out loud, "To keep you safe. Rocánonom sent us to travel with you. He knows you are tracking Kurnan, but so does the Malevir."

The escarpment shuddered as Enderfon stepped off the ledge, bounded down the slope, and reached the base of the rockwall. "Enough talk," he said, turning to look up at his visitors. "I spotted Kurnan. He'll reach the uprooters' pond soon. If you want him alive, you'd better come down from there and follow me."

Draako's warm snout nudged Nnylf's shoulder. *Up you go, friend. No time to lose.*

Alana mounted her dragon, and Isabella leaped with grace from the ledge.

What a waste of time. Kurnan will fight to keep the amulet, and we have no wish to harm him. Besides... He watched Alana hunker into the wind. *I don't want Alana hurt, either*

As Nnylf turned to climb Draako's extended leg, his dragon grunted. "The Malevir knows we are following Kurnan. He will use every spell he can to keep us from taking the amulet, even kill us if we stand in his way."

"Then shouldn't we give up? What's the point?"

Draako snorted a blast of cinders and dark smoke. "Give up? Not possible. We will take the amulet away from Kurnan."

"How?"

"We'll find help. I'm sure of it. Mount up. We have a long, tough journey ahead of us."

Nnylf tugged at Draako's neck frill as he settled into the dragon's rider's hump. "I'll do as you say, Draako." *If it makes sense.*

"I heard that," Draako bellowed as he sprang into the air.

SWEETNETTLE

CLINGING TO ENDERFON'S SHOULDER, Sweetnettle looked coldside and saw a broad frozen pond not far ahead. He picked out someone in the distance, between the pond and the mountains that loomed near the horizon. *That must be Kurnan. If we don't catch him now, he will escape into mountain caves and tunnels.*

Bemused, Sweetnettle startled as Enderfon whispered, "Not long now. I don't know how Kurnan escaped those uprooters. They hide in a hollow below that pond."

"The pond looks frozen and calm to me."

"Watch and stay here." He tapped Sweetnettle's perch with a fingertip. "No flying."

Sweetnettle's hearts fluttered again. The last time uprooters had crossed his path, he had been with his Loblin brothers, digging a tunnel into the Sunsetside Mountain. The sprites had entered an old passageway leading from the Coldside Desert into the Veiled Valley to hide from a bristle-toothed basilisk. Sweetnettle had never forgotten the beast's furious screams echoing far behind them as the Loblin dug in a frenzy of fear.

They escaped. Their tunnel's narrow opening blocked the basilisk. Relieved and weary from their efforts, the Loblin laid down their tools and rested against the damp tunnel walls. Small glowing orbs they pulled from their sacks cast a dim light through the tunnel. The Loblin settled in to chew on cakes.

After they had eaten and settled in for a nap, the Loblin heard thuds coming from a side passageway. Sweetnettle also recognized peculiar low growls and snuffling. Signaling his fellow Loblin to stay quiet, Sweetnettle held out an orb and tiptoed down the passageway. He froze when dim shadows around a bend of the tunnel moved toward him. An awful smell turned his stomach—sour, wet wool and rotting leaves—the stench of uprooters, furry, slouching beasts—ancestors of the Loblin—now under a painful Malevir spell.

Sweetnettle's band of sprites packed their gear and ran through another ancient tunnel until they were sure both basilisks and uprooters were far, far away from them.

Sweetnettle sighed. If only he could have broken the spell the uprooters suffered then, but there'd been no time.

Cold, damp drops were tickling Sweetnettle's nose. *Snow! Oh, no. Not now. How can we keep sight of Kurnan in a snowstorm? What if Enderfon is right? Will we see uprooters? Can I help them this time?*

Riding Enderfon's shoulder was like bobbing among heaving waves in Rocánonom's ship. Up and down, rising and falling, with each step the giant swayed and lurched. Sweetnettle crouched and clung to a stony knob jutting from Enderfon's neck. Each of the giant's strides jostled the Lobli, and his belly heart bumped against his rib cage. Buffeted by gusts of wind and sleet, he shivered in the cold and massaged his shoulder heart. *Don't flutter now, my friend. Belly heart can't do this alone.*

He heard a flapping sound, like sails caught in fierce Coldside Sea winds. The dragons were flying ahead, their broad bat wings propelling them upwards, above the snowstorm clouds. Why were they racing ahead? Moments later, with a burst of speed, they broke through cloud cover over the pond and swooped close to its frozen surface. Crimson dragon flames reflected off the pond's surface. Sweetnettle winced at splotches of red light filling his sight. He gripped the rock knob and squeezed his eyes shut.

Enderfon's sudden halt startled Sweetnettle. He rubbed his eyelids with his knuckles. Where were they? The giant was standing on the pond's shore. Sweetnettle looked across the swirling water. The dragons' flames died down, and a large bubble of water swelled at the pond's center. Enderfon's voice was as loud as a waterfall's cascade. "You stay put now, little fellow. Something fearsome is coming."

The pond's bubble broke, and the dragons flew up to circle above it. Hunched beasts rose out of the bubble and lumbered toward the giant. Their soggy fur dripped as they lifted their thick legs out of the water. Draako dived toward them. Smoke billowed from his jaws. Nnylf was steadying his short lance and looked ready to launch it at an uprooter leading the pack.

"Stop, stop!" Sweetnettle called out. "Do not kill them!"

The uprooters huddled together. At Sweetnettle's cry, they began to sink.

"Do not leave, brothers!" Sweetnettle called out. The uprooters raised their heads, and Sweetnettle gasped as he saw the sadness in their deep, weeping eyes.

"Brothers?" Enderfon boomed. "Hardly."

"You are mistaken. Giant friend, put me down!" Sweetnettle called to Nnylf and the giant, "Come close so you can hear me! The uprooters are spellbound and we must help them!"

The beasts sank lower. With arms wrapped around each other, they disappeared once more into the dark pond water. The two young riders urged their dragons to land by Enderfon's feet. Isabella tossed her head, agitated, seeming determined to blast the pond with her flames. Alana stroked her frill and crooned to her until the Copper quieted.

Isabella stretched her back legs, knelt, and settled into the snow. "Very well, Sweetnettle." She sighed. "But why not kill them? Uprooters prey on wyrmlings. They tear them to pieces and eat them before the little ones have a chance to grow into dragonets."

"How do you know that?" Sweetnettle asked. "Did you ever see them eat a wyrmling?"

"Well, no, but my mother told me…"

"These sad creatures are not what they seem. Since we don't know how to break the spell, we'll ask Aurykk."

"Break what spell?" asked Nnylf.

"The Malevir turned them into uprooters. Your lance would have killed an UrLobli, the most ancient kind of sprite in our land and all of the Beyond."

"They scare me," Alana said as she tightened her cloak around her shoulders. "They don't look like you or any of the valley Loblin."

Sweetnettle cleared his throat. He was unaccustomed to making long speeches. "UrLoblin dug out the first tunnels running under the Veiled Valley and through the mountains. The Malevir captured them to dig nests for basilisks in the Coldside Desert. He cast a spell, and they sprouted long, hard digging claws, thick tangled fur, and eyes that see in the dark. Rumor is that a few of them still live in the mountain tunnels. I saw some there, but long ago."

Alana said, "Uh, well, I never heard of UrLoblin until now. Hope you're right about these creatures. Oh, look, I think Aurykk and our dragons are sharing thoughts." She was facing the dark water where Isabella was standing nose to nose with Draako on the shore. The eyes of both dragons were closed. Blue smoke wafted over their heads and formed a long thin line that looped the pond.

Enderfon placed a hand by his own shoulder and wiggled a finger. "Jump on, Sweetnettle. You come up now."

Sweetnettle shook his head and remained near the dragonriders. Enderfon heaved a sigh that sounded like wind rising before a storm.

Nnylf slipped his weapon into a carrying strap while he and Alana watched their dragons.

"What are they doing?" Nnylf asked.

Sweetnettle wasn't sure. "Sometimes when dragons touch snouts, they share powers. Maybe they are talking to Aurykk. Look, shouldn't we send a message to Rocánonom?"

Sweetnettle became aware of a sound. *Tweetle-chirp*. Birdsong! He looked around and pulled on Nnylf's sleeve. "Look, it's the chary bird, my little messenger. Must have wriggled out of Isabella's jaw pouch."

Nnylf squatted and offered the little bird his open palm, salted with crumbs of barley cake. The chary bird hopped onto Nnylf's hand, feasted on the crumbs, and raised one leg.

Sweetnettle giggled. "She thinks we're going to wrap another message around her leg."

"Well, aren't we?" said Alana.

Sweetnettle's belly heart bumped his throat. Of course they were! "What should I write?"

"Tell Rocánonom we've found uprooters and need to break the Malevir's spell over them. Aurykk and our dragons are sharing thoughts. What can we do?"

"Sounds good." Sweetnettle pulled a scrap of bark paper from his pouch. Once he finished writing, he tied the message to the chary bird's leg and sent his courier winging off to Rocánonom's tower.

Nnylf turned to Alana. "What if the uprooters come out of the pond? We can't let our dragons hurt them."

Alana rested her hand on his arm and squeezed. "They won't. You know they hear everything we think or say."

"I hope not everything and not right now," Nnylf answered in a low voice. He looked into her eyes and held her hand.

Sweetnettle looked from one dragonrider to the other and back again. *Hmmm, maybe you two...* He shook his head with a smile.

But no. Enderfon scooped him up and perched him on his shoulder. Doffing his cap and calling to the young man and woman, Sweetnettle waved but they did not notice.

KURNAN

THE MEETING OF MOUNTAINS loomed over him. After his long trek across the frozen valley, Kurnan longed to rest. He ached to lie on the hard ground, but the voices shrieked whenever his eyelids drooped. Pain pierced his head from one ear to the other until he went on. Only now, as he gazed at the great gap between two mountain ranges, did the pain subside and the voices whisper, *Go through the pass.*

"What?" Kurnan mumbled, his lips numb with cold and hunger.

You must cross. To the Coldside Desert.

"Why there?"

There. Your new home.

"How soon?"

Silence.

"I asked you how soon?"

No answer. The moon rose over the gap, illuminating a silvery path over a rugged trail. Kurnan turned his head slowly for one last look at the Veiled Valley. In the distance, the lights of Fossarelick glimmered through the valley's evening mists, and his heart knotted. He remembered a bowl of steaming porridge cupped in his mother's calloused hands. As a lone tear settled in a corner of his eye, the stabbing pain returned. Kurnan turned his back on the valley and began his trek up to the moonlit trail.

He followed the winding path up a gentle slope. The moon was high in the sky when he reached a narrow gorge, bordered by outcroppings and boulders silhouetted against the glowing sky. Some looked like misshapen beasts; others resembled frowning giants or horks. His feet slipped on loose gravel. *Did that boulder move?* His breath shortened, and cold sweat trickled across his cheeks. Kurnan was afraid to move on.

DRAAKO

ISABELLA WAS CLAWING HIS snout. Her bright green eyes urged him to look at a tiny figure flying toward them. Their friend the chary bird zigzagged, buffeted by the snowstorm raging around them. She beat her wings with fierce energy until she fluttered to a spot between the dragons. Closing her eyes, the tiny bird rested her beak on the ground and tucked her legs under her breast.

"Night is nearly on us, but our steadfast messenger returns. Nnylf, please untie the scroll from her leg and read it to us," Draako said.

Nnylf gently patted his dragon's foreleg. "That I will, Draako." He stroked the bird's head and held out a palmful of barley bread crumbs. After the chary bird lifted her head and pecked at Nnylf's offering, Sweetnettle sat next to her. The bird sighed and lowered her head once more. Sweetnettle wrapped her in a red rag. Cooing a lullaby, he cuddled the bird and sang her to sleep. Only then did Nnylf uncover her leg, undo the intricate knots, and remove the note.

Alana tapped her foot and crossed her arms over her chest. "What does it say, Nnylf? Rocánonom must have an answer. He has a—" She clapped her hands over her mouth.

"Go on," Draako urged her as his own smoke drifted into his

eyes. He coughed. "What does he have that can help us?" He knew
Rocánonom well, a Forest Protector who had befriended valley dragons over countless World-Turns. When the Malevir had destroyed
nearly all the dragon clans around the Veiled Valley, the giant and
his Loblin had somehow found ways to undo the beast's enchantments and help defeat Aindle, the Malevir's aiglonax. Now many
dragons, of all colors and abilities, inhabited Dragonwolder again.

Alana looked across the pond, then shrugged. "Rocánonom has
many suggestions, I am sure. Read his message, please."

Nnylf looked at her, raising an eyebrow, and Alana blushed.

Sweetnettle nodded, cleared his throat, and read: "Your dragons
must circle and send their thoughts to Aurykk."

"We did that, we're still waiting for his reply," grumbled Isabella.
"What else?"

Sweetnettle nodded. "He writes: 'Aurykk knows helpful enchantments and—'"

"What enchantments?"

"Please, everyone. Let me finish," Sweetnettle pleaded.

Isabella bit her lip and mumbled quietly to herself. "I'm only
asking..."

"'...Isabella and Draako, listen for Aurykk's message. If you hear
it and follow his instructions, soon you will meet long-lost UrLoblin.'" Sweetnettle dropped the message, and the wind picked it up
and tossed it into the pond. It floated for a few moments then sank.

Draako lifted his head and turned away from his cousin. Nnylf
and Alana stood close to each other. The young man was pointing to
Enderfon's upper body. Draako only caught a few of his rider's words:
"What did Rocánonom..." and "Can't you tell me..." and "very well."
Nnylf shrugged and turned away from Alana.

Draako sighed. "Whichever of us first hears from Aurykk, let
the other know. I'm going to nap until he sends his thoughts." The
Copper nodded then curled around him and soon fell asleep. Draako

draped his wings over his head after settling his snout on his forelegs. Jagged snores filled the air.

ALANA

AFTER BLOWING WILDLY, THE snowstorm ended and the night sky cleared. Draako and Isabella, exchanging puffs of cinder-dotted smoke, hunched and pressed into each other. The Copper coughed and raised her head above Draako's. As she shook off melting clumps of snow, she thundered, "There it is, Aurykk's message."

Alana sat bolt upright. She and Nnylf had fallen asleep in the crook of the rock giant's elbow. Her sudden movement jostled Nnylf, and he began to roll over the edge of Enderfon's arm. With both hands, she grabbed her friend's leg. The young man opened one eye and grinned at her.

Her pulse quickening, Alana stifled a nervous giggle. Her cheeks were burning. What did his grin mean? She turned away and asked Enderfon to put them on the ground.

Ever watchful, Enderfon blared. "Careful, now! You're not made of stone, you know." Alana was all too aware of that as side by side she and Nnylf worked their way down his arm. Jumping off the giant's finger tips, she ran to her dragon.

With eyes closed and long, rugged jaws agape, Draako and Isabella stood at each other's side, swaying back and forth as if they were listening to a steady drum beat. *Drums!* Alana thought, *I do hear drumming.*

"Their hearts are beating so loud," Nnylf whispered. "I hope they don't explode." His jaw tightened. "They must have picked up a message from Aurykk."

Alana swung her attention back to Isabella, whose forelegs lay stretched out in front of her on the packed snow. The Copper folded her back legs like a resting cat and stared across the pond's still water. Was she sick? Alana started to call her, but Nnylf tugged at her elbow.

"Don't. Can't you see that both dragons are building their strength?"

"What do you mean?"

"That's what Aurykk and the other Orferans did before they led their dragon flokk against the aiglonax."

"How does it work?"

"To gather their strength, they sit close like that. If we were closer to them, you'd hear their hearts hum between beats. They're connecting to the Mystic Scintilla. They hum until its ancient powers fill every part of them. I saw it happen long ago."

"What's next then?"

"When ready, they will take action."

No sooner had Nnylf said "action" than Isabella and Draako arched their backs, whipped their tails, and began to torch the pond. Alana stumbled back as the heat of their flames sent billows of steam into the air. She turned to run from the scalding vapor but, wedged between two sharp-cornered fingers, she rose above it. Enderfon was holding Nnylf in his other hand. The giant took a few strides backward and held the two riders over his head. Alana begged him to bring them closer. She wanted to stop their dragons from destroying the UrLoblin; both dragons were deaf to her calls.

Enderfon's cupped hands caged the two dragonriders. High above the fire's glare, Alana heard nothing but the roar of flames and the hiss of evaporating water. Feeling as if a cartload of barley sheaves sat on her shoulders, she curled into a ball. Through unbidden tears, she gazed at clouds of stars drifting through the inky sky overhead. Her eyelids itched. She closed her eyes, intending to rest for a few moments.

$\sim$

At first, she heard chirps. Opening her eyes to the soft light of sunrising, Alana smiled at the chary bird sitting on her shoulder. Below her, the dragons were sleeping on the shore of the drained pond bed. Bodies of silvery fish lay strewn across muddy flats, among twisted and shriveled lengths of scorched pond weed. In the middle scrooched a huddle of shivering, soggy uprooters. Still alive! They held each other close. Some were wailing; others covered their eyes with matted paws as they rocked side to side.

Sweetnettle shared Alana's stony perch. The chary bird hopped between the two of them. The Lobli squeaked, "Now that the sky is clear, the chary bird would like to return to Rocánonom and his sweet cakes. I'll wake the dragons. They have one more step to save the uprooters. That done, I can send this little messenger back." Sweetnettle squeezed from between Enderfon's fingers and jumped. His lacy wings carried him fluttering onto Isabella's snout.

That's leaping into the heat of things, Alana thought.

I heard that, Isabella answered, one green-rimmed amber eye popping open. Sweetnettle landed next to Isabella's long, pointed ear. He bent into the ear's opening and held his hands around his mouth. "Isabella, now for the real magick?" he shouted.

"What did you say?" Isabella roared and Sweetnettle somersaulted backward before his wings carried him safely to the ground.

The Copper's upper lip curled in a fang-filled smile. "Just teasing. I know, you're right. Draako and I must complete the spell-break. Thank you for the reminder."

Sweetnettle bowed. His wings shimmered like a dragonfly's in the sun as he flitted back to the rock giant. Alana held out her arms. The Lobli flew up then settled into her lap, and his warmth spread through her armor and across her belly.

Nnylf was dozing in Enderfon's other hand. Alana wanted him to share the sight of great dragon magick. "Wake up, Nnylf. You're missing all the excitement."

The young man rubbed his sleepy eyes. "What? Where?" he mumbled, looking up and around.

"Down there."

Sweetnettle hiccupped, and Alana could feel the rapid beat of his belly heart. She tightened her arms around him—but not too much. With wide eyes, they both watched the dragons' conjuration.

Draako and Isabella raised their heads and opened their jaws as if they meant to drink in the morning's sunbeams. They began to purr so loudly that any nearby cat would have fled in fear. Their thrumming sent wafts of icy mist around the cluster of uprooters. Soon, the dragons' hum became a chant:

> Malevir done
> Rivelam undone
> Uprooters rebel
> To unravel the spell
> Your new life begun
> Old life farewell

The song continued to throb all around them and through Enderfon's stony core. Alana's limbs felt long and soft, soothed by the song's calming rhythm. She struggled to keep her eyes on the uprooters. Those annoying mists, so like the Veiled Valley, hiding exactly what you wanted to see. She could hardly hear the dragons' chanting anymore, as if the mists had packed her ears with woolen batting.

The moment the dragons' incantation stopped, the mists cleared. Scanning the pond bed for uprooters, Alana saw a pile of squirming little bodies, stacked in a mound, where the uprooters had been huddling. Pity filled her eyes with tears. How miserable they looked! What horrors had they known?

Draako reached them first, and Isabella was close behind him. The creatures wailed and groaned from fear as much as from the mess of their tangled arms and legs. "Don't move!" the Silver roared.

They squealed.

Draako's roar roused Nnylf. He stretched his arms and rubbed his eyes. "What's happening? Where are the uprooters?"

"Don't you see? Look over there," Alana shouted. "In the middle of the pond. Must you sleep through everything?"

"Well, no, but the heat…the chanting…made me so sleepy."

Alana regretted her harsh words and smiled at her friend. "I'm sorry. I fell asleep, too."

Draako softened his voice. "Enderfon, please bring Nnylf and Alana here and, Sweetnettle, will you prepare another message for the chary bird?"

Enderfon crouched and opened his palms. Alana and Nnylf slid to the ground. "Ouch!" Nnylf cried when he stepped onto the dry pond bed. "It's hot! We can't walk on it."

"Enderfon is bringing some snow and ice to make a path for you and the UrLoblin."

"Good idea, Draako." Nnylf smirked. "Meanwhile, the uprooters are cooking."

"No," Alana said. "Isabella has packed a ring of icy slush around them. Oh, my, they don't look like uprooters anymore. They don't look like anything I know, covered in mud like that."

In fact, the shivering mass of creatures was half the size of the uprooters' huddle. Those with free arms were scooping up handfuls of slush and rubbing it over their bodies.

Enderfon's gleaming snow path stretched from the shore to the transformed uprooters. Walls of steam rose on either side of the path and arched overhead to form a heated tunnel. Before Alana could stop him, Sweetnettle darted under the misty vault and flew toward the huddle. She lost sight of him until he emerged near the shore, a line of creatures trudging after him out of the pond.

Nnylf and Alana met them with a bundle of red rags Sweetnettle had given them. They followed Isabella's instructions to dip the rags in melted snow puddles on shore. While Alana prepared her first rag, Isabella called out, "Take the hand of the first creature you meet! Let your rag drip all over him. Squeeze the rag's last bit of water over his head. Bring him to me after you tie the rag around his neck. Nnylf, you do the same. Remember to chant:

> 'Uprooters rebel
> To unravel the spell
> Your new life begun
> Rivelam farewell'"

One of the creatures left the line and shuffled toward Alana. The uprooter's approach made her queasy. Alana stumbled back, but the creature's odd appearance puzzled her. This uprooter didn't look so fierce. Mud-matted fuzz covered the top of its head, and it had draped a rag around its middle. Half her height, it moved with a dancing grace as it neared her. Splotches of dirt hid most of its face, and no fangs stuck out of its little mouth. The thing slowly lifted one arm and held out a hand, not a clawed uprooter paw.

Alana stepped closer. Her curiosity moved her to chant Isabella's words while squeezing water over the creature's head. Alana then scrubbed its open palm, three fingers, and very long thumb.

She heard tinkling laughter and "Oh, ha! That's good!" She lowered her head to meet the uprooter's gaze. The creature's bright eyes were the color of sea water and dotted with gold flecks. She greeted Alana with a rivulet of giggles, revealing rows of even white teeth in a wide, fern-green grin. Green! Just like Sweetnettle.

Alana dabbed more water on the creature's shivering shoulders and arms then wiped away the last specks of dirt on her new acquaintance's face.

She whispered, "I am Alana. Who are you?"

"Good. I am very much Good."

"Happy to hear that, but I asked what is your name?"

"My name is Good. Happy is over there. We are UrLoblin." She pointed to the creature Nnylf was helping.

"Thank you, Good. I think I'm beginning to understand, but what are UrLoblin?"

Good patted her hand. "Ancestors of your Loblin, like Sweetnettle." She flicked a long finger at mud still clinging to one elbow.

"Let me help you." Repeating the chant, Alana scrubbed Good's arms and legs with more puddle water. Good gently tugged the rag from her and rolled in the puddle's deepest part. She crouched and used the rag to splash water all over herself until no mud remained.

The seven other UrLoblin held out their hands for a rag. After they finished bathing, Good skipped from puddle to puddle and spoke to her companions in low tones. Then she stood shivering on packed snow. With heads bowed, they hugged each other and huddled again.

Isabella and Draako rescued them from the cold. Hovering over the UrLoblin, they heated the air with a soft cloud of sparkling vapor. The UrLobin's eyes widened, their shoulders stiffened and, raising their heads, they let out a collective whistle when they saw the dragons who had frightened them with roaring fire.

Alana's thoughts flew to Isabella. *I hope they're not afraid. They must have known your dragon ancestors in the earliest times, before the Malevir enchanted them.*

They will not fear us after today.

"I'm happy to hear that," Alana said aloud.

"No," squeaked Good. "This is Happy." She pointed to the UrLobli standing at her side.

"Um, I see. I'll say it another way: I feel like jumping for joy because you are free."

Good nodded to Alana with a smile. "We thank you, but don't jump for Joy. See her there?" A fluffy UrLobli waved, spun on her toes, and jumped into the air before bowing in a curtsey. Masses of red curls fell forward and covered Joy's face.

Sweetnettle drifted down from Enderfon's shoulder and spoke to them. "Welcome. We're so hap—er, feeling good—no, I mean—welcome! I sent a message to the giant Rocánonom thanking him for helping us. Of course, the real magick came from another dragon you might remember, the wise elder Aurykk."

The UrLoblin clapped their hands. "Aurykk! Oh, yes. Is he well? Please tell us more." Good giggled. All eight UrLoblin squatted to listen.

"He is well. And you remember Rocánonom? Then you will not fear this big fellow, the rock giant Enderfon of the Warmside Beyond. He helped us free you from the pond and the Malevir's spell. Without him, we might never have succeeded."

Enderfon rose from where he was sitting, as motionless as a rocky outcropping. As he approached the group, his shadow fell over them, and eight faces filled with wonder.

"It really is you, Enderfon!" Happy shouted. "We thought the Malevir killed…but, never mind. You are safe."

"Not so much as I'd like," thundered Enderfon.

Good's forehead puckered, and she tightened her mouth. "Why not safe? What do you fear?"

"I'm not afraid, but I see signs of the Malevir's bad magick wherever I go."

"Oh, no! Everywhere? Even here? We can't let the Malevir find us and hurt us again. We must leave—now!!" Good shrieked.

Sweetnettle kicked at clumps of snow and rubbed his belly heart. "Please calm yourselves. Stay with us," he whispered. "We'll protect you."

Good flicked the frost collecting on her fuzz. "So kind of you, but there's something else: we are terribly cold. Would dear Sweetnettle have something in his pouch to keep us warm? You can see the Malevir stole our garments." The other UrLoblin tittered and, plucking at the damp rags wrapped around their bellies, they huddled closer to each other.

Enderfon replied, "I, too, ask you not to leave us. Sweetnettle will give you warm cloaks to last the rest of this Cold-Turn. You will find comfort with us."

"He's right. Why all this talk of leaving?" said Nnylf. "We've just met, and I'd like to know more about you." He stood shoulder to shoulder with Alana and exchanged a quick glance with her. "They're taller than Sweetnettle," he whispered. "Up to here." And he pointed to his waist.

Alana nodded then turned away. Something about Nnylf's look made her feel funny, as if she were floating. Her cheeks were burning. She didn't want to think about Nnylf's waist right then. She shook her head to banish the thought. "Keep talking. Make them stay. We could use their help."

Nnylf frowned then turned to the UrLoblin. "I speak for all of us. Stay with us. We have ties to the strongest magick in the Veiled Valley and the Beyonds. It will keep you safe."

Happy's three slender fingers fluffed her curls. "You'll be in big trouble if we UrLoblin travel with you. The Malevir will see us. He will come for us. He will attack. By leaving, we protect *you*. No, no, we cannot stay."

Isabella drifted to the ground. "Loblin, we freed you. You owe us your pledge to help us if we call you. I am Isabella, daughter of Serpinafria. Honor me with your promise."

The UrLoblin murmured and nodded.

"Long ago, during the old World-Turns, you knew my mother. Moktawl hunters from Fossarelick killed her after the Malevir poisoned their hearts."

The UrLoblin gasped.

"Dragons like me survived the Malevir and the Moktawls. We lived in hiding. After dragonriders persuaded valley folk to trust us again, as in the old times, we fought the Malevir together. We destroyed him, or so we thought. At least we put an end to his creature, the aiglonax Aindle."

Draako spoke up, "But not the Malevir himself. Now we track his new tool, a young man. The beast's bad magick holds him captive. The man is making his way toward the Meeting of Mountains, where we hope to stop him."

The UrLoblin talked among themselves. Squeaking and burbling, they shrugged, hopped, and twirled. Finally, bowing deeply, Good said, "Friends, your words make our hearts thump and we are sad to leave you, but it's for the best. We must return to the UrLoblin tunnels we built long ago. They twist and turn coldside before winding under the Meeting of Mountains, where we made our last home. Warmed by the cloaks you give us, we will begin our journey."

Happy whispered a few bubbling sounds into Good's pointed ear, and Good nodded. "Sorry. How could I be so rude? We thank you again; you reawakened our spirits and we won't forget you. Perhaps, you will meet and help others of our kind. Now, we return underearth to our home."

Good's speech made Alana miserable. With the UrLoblin's help, the trackers might have found other ways to free Kurnan from the Malevir's spell. She tried not to think of her brother's pain and anger, but it weighed on her. "Please change your minds."

Enderfon interrupted, "They can't, so we'll have to do this." Enderfon raised his shining mace. The UrLoblin huddled and cried out, "Don't hurt us!"

The giant shook his head and pointed Rowel at Sweetnettle's pouch, lying in the snow. He mumbled one of his strange-sounding enchantments and stepped back.

Sweetnettle gulped and the UrLoblin crept forward. The pouch was ballooning. Its flap snapped open. Woolen cloaks spilled out— pairs of blue, red, yellow, and pale green cloaks, followed by boots, leggings, shirts, and small sacks that hummed when the UrLoblin picked them up.

Snug in their warm garb, the UrLoblin patted their new sacks and bowed. Good stepped forward. "We cannot promise to help, but the time might come. Our love to Rocánonom. Rivelam undone. New life begun." She turned away.

Beneath the UrLoblin's feet, cracks spread across the glassy snow in a widening circle. With a wink to Sweetnettle, the sprites stood at the edge of the circle and repeated, *Rivelam undone. New life begun.*

A small opening at the center of the circle began to grow, brightened by a soft glowing light. Good left her companions and peered into it. "Nothing has changed since we left it. Come, sisters and brothers. To underearth and to home."

As they disappeared into the hole, Alana ran to its edge and nearly fell in as she called out, "Wait, wait, you forgot to tell us how to find—" but she never had the chance to finish her sentence.

PART 3

MOUNTAIN MENACE

UPROOTER.

KURNAN

WEARY FROM HIS SLOG up the snow-covered slope, Kurnan shifted from one aching foot to the other before stepping into a dark gorge, robbed of the blue moonlight lighting the path behind him. The gorge walls leaned inward, as if poised to smother him under a rockfall. His chest tightened as the cold night air burned his throat.

The cave will shelter you.

Anger heated his face. "What cave? I can't see anything but rocks that look like trolls."

Over there.

Kurnan saw a flickering light a few steps ahead of him. It floated away and into a deep hollow. The light led to a rock shelter. He sighed with relief—this would be a good place to pass the rest of the night, but only if the voices were silent and he could sleep. He entered the hollow. Under the faint light floating overhead, he looked for a place to lie down.

His knee hit the edge of a long, flat block of stone. Kurnan rubbed at the sudden new pain and looked down. The block would do as a bed. Brushing off debris scattered over the surface, he sat down, crossed his legs under himself, and opened his sack. He rummaged through it, although he knew his own supplies were gone. His hand wrapped around the water gourd. He shook it—empty. Next to it lay a strange red pod. He had a hazy memory of drinking something delicious from it. Draining it, in fact. Surely, no drink remained. When he shook it, he heard something slosh inside.

Thank the Ways of the World. Something to drink. Kurnan pried off the pod's seal and gulped the liquid gushing out of it. *A mix of honey, toasted bread, and sweet cheese.* He shook the pod again to eke out the last drop, but when he raised it to his lips, another gush of sweet nectar filled his mouth. He lay back on the flat stone and fell into a deep sleep.

Before sunrising, Kurnan was awake. His growling stomach reminded him of the pod. Frantic, he patted and swept the stone bed and cave floor with his hands, blindly groping for his only hope of food. When his eyes adjusted to the faint magical light still floating overhead, he found the pod at the foot of the stone. He drank deeply.

He licked his lips. *Thank the Ways of the World, if They care about me. They might. Maybe They gave me this pod. Maybe They want me to be here, free from Fossarelick.*

Kurnan drank until he could drink no more. Sated, he threw the pod into his sack. The amulet started to burn his chest, and one of his voices barked, *Leave here. You're almost home.* Startled, Kurnan tripped and dropped his sack.

"Home? Not Fossarelick?" He groaned.

No, your new safe place.

"How do I find it?"

The silver path will take you there.

Kurnan looked outside the shelter. The blizzard had moved on. Walking out into bright sunlight, he saw two mountain ranges. As a boy, they had made him feel so small and powerless. Now the voices' power and magick protected him. Past the gorge and beyond the cleft between the mountains lay a bright path, bordered by high walls of newly fallen snow. Kurnan could not resist it. Freedom and the end of pain waited for him there.

NNYLF

COLD MOONLIGHT LAY ACROSS the ice flats ahead of them as Nnylf and Draako flew toward the Meeting of Mountains. Nnylf's chest tightened at the sight of peaks looming in the distance. They were near the place where, many World-Turns ago, a violent mountain storm had tossed and battered him and Draako. Beset by whirlwinds and crackling thunderbolts, Draako had swooped and darted out of the storm to bring Nnylf to safety in the Anonom Trace. Later he and Draako joined with dragon flokks to plot a stronger defense against the Malevir. Now he and Draako were approaching the same mountain pass.

Isabella was flying quite close to Draako. Her strong, leathery copper wings beat a slow, pulsing rhythm as they soared across frozen tarns and snowbound dales.

Nnylf leaned toward the Copper and, hoping the fitful gusts buffeting them would not steal his words, he yelled, "How can we catch up to Kurnan? I don't see him. And where is Enderfon?"

Alana pointed to her own ears then patted Isabella's head.

The Copper relayed Alana's thoughts. *Your words vanished in the wind. What did you say? Ah, finding Kurnan.*

Yes. He's disappeared.

But I know where he's gone, said Draako.

Nnylf asked, *How? Can you see him?*

No, but Isabella and I both feel the way the air quivers when something of the Malevir is near.

Isabella added, *When the amulet is close, I feel its power. Are you worried about our rock giant friend?*

A little sick from Draako's sudden dips and turns, Nnylf slowly nodded.

Don't fret. He's not far.

Nnylf gripped Draako's frill with one hand and twisted to catch sight of Enderfon. He smiled with relief when he realized that an oddly shaped outcrop on the flats was moving in their direction. Enderfon had fallen behind his companions, but not by much. Nnylf hoped that Sweetnettle still rode the giant's rough shoulder as he lumbered across the icy wasteland.

Nnylf heard the dragons calling the giant with comforting words and directions. They were going to land on high flat ground, halfway up the slopes, between the mountain ranges. There, they would set up camp and wait until the amulet betrayed Kurnan's next stop.

Alana and Nnylf eagerly slid off their dragons as soon as Isabella's and Draako's huge legs touched the ground. Landing feet first, they whooped in surprise as they plunged into a waist-high snowdrift. Their laughter mixed with shrieks when they realized they were stuck. Draako pulled them out and shot a volley of small flames over another part of the rock shelf. They stood shivering on the warm, dry spot until Draako's flames revealed a small shelter in the rock wall. It looked like a shallow cave. The Silver's fire melted all the snow surrounding the cave. It trickled over the edge of the shelf and formed icicles.

Isabella opened her long jaws. She pulled a bundle out of her jaw pouch and laid it on the newly-dry shelter floor. "Everything you need is here. Except food. Sweetnettle will bring you something to eat, I am sure. When Enderfon arrives."

Nnylf stopped chafing his arms and knelt next to the bundle. He sorted its contents: flints and kindling, coverlets and straw, the makings of a torch, cups, two horn combs, and a handful of red rags.

While they waited for the giant, Alana lit a torch and Nnylf followed her into the small cave. The torch light illuminated a broad, flat rock, swept clean of debris, as if someone had used it not long ago. Nnylf asked Alana to bring the torch closer to a small red object on the floor. He poked it then picked it up.

"Wonder what this is." He juggled it in his palm.

Alana shrugged. "I guess it's one of Sweetnettle's pods. The Lobli said he left one with Kurnan before we arrived at the red needlerock."

"So he was here." The thought chilled Nnylf, despite the dragons' warming their shelter. Uneasy, he turned away from the slab. *What else had Kurnan left behind. Spells? Traps? Was his old friend now another of the Malevir's creatures?*

He stepped outside the rock shelter and hurled the pod over some distant boulders. His hands felt dirtied and he tried to rub them clean. *Who knows what the Malevir did to Kurnan? Maybe that pod carried more bad magick that could hurt Alana.* Regretting he'd left her alone, Nnylf hurried back inside the rock shelter.

Torch light bathed a far section of the wall where Alana was crouching next to strange marks carved into its surface. She traced a line of marks with her finger. "What do you think this is?"

Nnylf hoped she hadn't heard his sigh of relief. *She's fine. Good.* "I don't know. Maybe Isabella can help." He called the Copper Dragon.

Isabella lowered her head to peek into the small cave. She stared at the marks and said, "Uprooters were here."

"Our uprooters? The UrLoblin?"

Isabella withdrew her head and touched snouts with Draako. Pale smoke spiraled above their heads as they shared their thoughts.

Finally, Isabella answered. "We can't be sure, but the Malevir's presence is strong here—or was. Kurnan's, too."

Nnylf searched Alana's eyes. They were dark with anger. Her hands were tight fists, knuckles butting each other. What was she thinking? If only he could find the right hopeful words she needed. Maybe the marks on the wall would give him a clue, some way to understand the Malevir's plans for Kurnan.

KURNAN

MELTED SNOW FAILED TO satisfy Kurnan's thirst. He dragged his legs up the mountain path and rubbed his growling belly. "Will this night never end? I need water." He hoped the voices would answer him.

But nothing. Not a word. Instead, his old pain was creeping behind his ears and along the back of his neck. Kurnan rubbed his scalp and shook his head, but the pain only worsened. "Don't be angry. Let me rest a bit!" The pain in his head subsided a bit.

Rest.

"You're back. I suppose I should be grateful."

Rest. Drink.

Kurnan eased his pack off his back and leaned against a stone outcrop at the path's edge. As the sky brightened toward sunriseside, he found his gourd, but the never-empty pod was missing. He was sure he'd packed it. Panic set in. "I am going to die of hunger and thirst."

Shaking his head, Kurnan grimaced and stuffed the gourd into his sack. Handfuls of snow would have to do.

Now move.

Kurnan used his sleeve to wipe his mouth and set off again for the far side of the mountain pass. His legs and back ached but he pushed himself forward. "Listen, I'm starving and cold and so tired. I hate slipping on rockfalls of scree and squeezing between weird boulders. Come on, help me here. I only want to be in that safe place you promised me."

Kurnan heard nothing but the wind whistling down the trail; but his head pains had ebbed. Did that mean the voices were about to find him an easier path?

The amulet started to burn him through his tunic. "Why? What do you want of me now? I'm walking, can't you see?"

You are near the top. Do not stop again.

Nearly faint from thirst, Kurnan lifted his gaze—attached as it had been to each hard-won step. He approached the path's highest point as a sunrising covered the desert below in morning's first blush. On either side of him, the mountain slopes slanted up and away from the path. Ahead of him was the broad, open sky.

Do not stop.

Kurnan ignored the voice. *Is my thirst playing a trick on me? Is that the sound of running water?* A burbling mountain stream flowed down the slope to his right. *Yes, there it is.*

He squatted next to the stream, which raced across the path. Hesitating, he poked his finger into the stream. It was real. He knelt and dipped his mouth into the water. As it swirled around his head, he took great gulps. Coming up for air, he gasped and coughed, then he plunged his head in again.

Stop, Kurnan. Do not drink here.

His once-parched throat was now numb. He wiped drops of water from his chilled face. After filling his gourd, he sat on a boulder and surveyed the area. Other than the murmur and splash of rushing water, the place looked calm and hushed. Kurnan closed his eyes and breathed in the sweet mountain air, smelling of wildflowers—and something else, something peppery, musky. He knew that smell.

He opened his eyes and searched the slope for its source—an animal smell, once part of his life in Fossarelick: the smell of a goat. A buck leaped over the rocky, uneven ground and down the slope. The goat's yellow eyes fixed on him. The closer he came, the stronger his stink, like everything foul in his family's animal pens with some old unwashed clothes thrown in.

The voice called him again. *Run. You are in danger.*

"Why? From what?"

Kurnan clambered to the top of a rock pile. What would a lone male goat be fleeing, froth flying from his mouth? Balancing on top of a broad rock, he searched the mountainside for trouble. He looked uphill and his heart clenched. Chasing the goat was a band of beasts, covered in long, shaggy fur. Uprooters! Thudding down the slope, they looked like the creatures he'd faced at the frozen pond.

Kurnan ducked behind a big reddish-brown rock, but too late. The uprooters spotted him and changed direction. Kurnan's stomach turned. He vomited stream water, took a deep breath, and jumped off the boulders onto the path. He was the uprooters' new quarry. The goat ran close behind him.

ROCÁNONOM

SNUG IN HIS TOWER, Rocánonom sat by his hearth. He read and reread every word of Sweetnettle's message:

Friend,

We did not capture the amulet—yet. Did free UrLoblin from Malevir's uprooter spell. They left us. Returned to underearth. Enderfon and his mace are strong. We follow Kurnan to the Meeting of Mountains.

Sweetnettle

The parchment nearly fell out of Rocánonom's shaking hand. Laying it with care on his worktable, he marveled to himself. Enderfon not only had his mace, but he was very much alive and able to use it. The young riders and his friend the giant were tracking Kurnan. What's more, they had found and freed UrLoblin! What else lay ahead?

He knew that his command of the Great Forces could help Sweetnettle and the others to capture Kurnan. Yet, the Malevir's power over the young man must be growing because of the amulet. It was feeding on Kurnan's anger and strengthening the Malevir's influence.

In his bones, Rocánonom knew a more favorable time would come to pit his own powers against the Malevir's. For now, and from a distance, he would help the trackers with advice. For now, from his high tower, he would continue to watch the Coldside Sea Island.

He smiled at the thought of Aurykk rummaging through his own store of spells, finding the right one to free their old friends the UrLoblin. But why did they return to the underearth? Surely other spellbound uprooters roamed through the tangle of tunnels running under the valley and through the mountains. What would happen if they met the freed UrLoblin? How Rocánonom wished he had been there, by the pond, to see them again and bind them to Enderfon and the others, but he shouldn't leave the tower, right?

Rocánonom circled his hearth, rubbed his smooth chin, and looked at his table. He relished the memory of the Elementals warming the Coldside Sea waters when he had to block Kurnan's path to the sea island. What ancient spell would he use to call the Elementals again to thwart the Malevir? He needed a stronger spell, one that would bind the Elementals to his commands. Would it be here among his pages? He rustled through the parchment sheets scattered across the table. Not this one. No, nor that.

Pressing his nose to another dusty sheet, Rocánonom mouthed the words of a spell so faded he could hardly read them. He shook his head in disgust. Where could the right spell be? He closed his eyes and took a deep breath.

His eyes snapped open. Of course! He'd seen it in the codex, the grimoire filled with Dragonwolder's most powerful spells, but if he took the book from its protected hiding place, the Malevir might find it. Everything would be lost. Anyway, he ought to remain in the tower and not endanger Aurykk.

No one except Aurykk knew of the grimoire's whereabouts, but the Golden did not know the exact spot. That knowledge was too dangerous to share. If only he could remember the spell. He paced around his hearth, and ashes and dust rose with every heavy footfall.

He had no choice. Sooner rather than later, he would need to leave his warm tower and make his way to the Cave of Refuge. Notes on the grimoire's spells, written in secret ciphers, filled the parchments spread across his table. None of them gave him the information he needed. Rocánonom muttered, "I must go, but when?" He paced the room then paused to look out the window.

SWEETNETTLE

ALTHOUGH THE ROCK GIANT offered Sweetnettle his shoulder, the Lobli said he preferred to sleep in a warmer place. He crept into the rock shelter unnoticed while Nnylf and Alana were inspecting the lines left in the wall by uprooters.

Nnylf cleared his throat. "Alana, how could beasts like uprooters leave such mysterious writing?"

Sweetnettle tugged at Alana's legging. "He's right. The Malevir must have chased UrLoblin to this spot. I think they wrote this and hoped someone would read it, maybe rescue them."

"Instead, the Malevir cast his spell and banished them to the pond?" Alana asked.

Sweetnettle didn't know how to answer her. Only eight UrLoblin had emerged from the pond. There must have been more.

"Some of them, I think. Not all."

Nnylf stood up and his head grazed the low cave ceiling. "Ouch." He patted the top of his head. "Well, I can't read this. How about you, Alana. No? Then we can't be sure."

Sweetnettle cast down his eyes. "I suppose you're right."

"So, Sweetnettle, you're saying more uprooters could be out there?" The crease between Nnylf's eyebrows deepened.

With a skip of his belly heart, Sweetnettle said, "I don't know, but we should be careful. I'll talk to Enderfon."

Musing over the markings, Sweetnettle flitted around outside until he bumped into a rock pillar. Before Sweetnettle had a chance to rub his bruised shoulder, Enderfon lifted him with a thumb and one finger until he was level with the giant's eyes.

"Enderfon, I was looking for you, but…"

The giant laughed. Sweetnettle's ears were ringing when Enderfon added, "I know, I know. A rock giant is hard to see in the dark."

"If I showed you old Loblin writing, could you tell me what it says?"

"No. Why?"

Sweetnettle's arms and legs were growing numb. His wings itched and he considered unfurling them again, but Enderfon must have sensed his discomfort. The giant returned him to the ground close to the rock shelter and squatted.

"Why?" Sweetnettle sighed. "Because Nnylf and Alana have found marks scratched into the shelter's wall. Come see."

Sweetnettle ran inside to have Alana throw as much light as she could on the wall. Enderfon's eyes were level with the opening to the shelter, and he squinted to have a better view of the marks. "You surprise me. I thought all Loblin had an inborn understanding of their ancestors' writing."

That wasn't fair. Someone had to teach us, and no UrLoblin were around when I was young, only uprooters. Our new UrLoblin friends should have stayed with us. They would know what the writing means. If only I knew the place they call home…

Sweetnettle fretted and stewed before he answered Enderfon. "None of my brothers or sisters ever saw UrLoblin marks like these. You have to be taught."

"Understood. Since I can't read the marks, I'll wake the dragons. Well, maybe only Draako. Isabella clings to her dreams. Draako will have a memory of UrLoblin writing somewhere in his brain or heart. It's there, wherever a dragon stores energy to command his mystical powers."

"Mystical powers…the ones given by the—"

"The Mystic Scintilla. Without that energy, they're only smart lizards. Come with me." Once more, Sweetnettle endured Enderfon's gentle squeeze. Snug in a rough but secure part of the giant's shoulder, he pulled his cap over his ears to guard against rising mountain winds. They found Draako and Isabella asleep on the sunriseside slope, high above the cave. Enderfon stopped, stood by Draako's nose, and lowered Sweetnettle onto a spine near the dragon's ear.

"Oh, Draako," Sweetnettle whispered, "forgive me, but…" He paused, took in a deep breath, and bellowed, "WAKE UP."

Sweetnettle fretted. The moon had set and a new sunrising would arrive soon. While they waited for Draako to unlock the meaning of the marks, Kurnan was getting away. He wondered how much longer the dragon would lie there with his head resting on his forelegs. The Silver stared at the rock wall but said nothing.

Sweetnettle's eyes itched. Wrapped in their cloaks, Nnylf and Alana remained asleep near the wall. How could they sleep? Wouldn't they want to hear Draako explain those strange gouges in the wall?

Draako cleared his throat and whispered, "Not long now. The marks will start to glow. My third eye is rearranging them into words." The marks closest to Nnylf began to brighten. As Draako stared, more marks glowed. At last, Draako blared, "Wake up, Nnylf and Alana! You should hear this too!"

The dragonriders flung off their cloaks and jumped to their feet. Dazed, they followed Sweetnettle out of the cave and sat cross-legged in front of Draako, who had pulled his head back outside. Isabella sat on her haunches next to Draako and Enderfon settled his mass behind the dragons, while Alana held Sweetnettle in a tight hug.

"Here it is, then." Draako coughed out a few cinders. "The marks are quite plainly UrLoblin and the meaning even plainer. They danced a bit before my eyes until my innermost heart chamber and third eye untangled them. I have to tell you—"

"Please, Draako, *do* tell us," Nnylf said, exasperated.

Draako's snout smoldered for a few moments and his eyes narrowed, but he seemed to shrug off the insult. "Of course, as I said, here it is."

> Long winter ends, as do we.
> Basilisks and the Beast chase us into the deep.
> Bodies no longer our own,
> Claws pushing out from the bone.
> Farewell dear home
> Hidden in the...

Draako fell silent and looked at each friend gathered around him. Then he sighed. "That's all."

Sweetnettle tore himself from Alana's arms and slid to the ground. Fluttering his wings, he hovered around Draako's snout. "What do you mean, 'That's all'? We must learn how to find their home. We'll need their help. After the words, 'Hidden in the...'?"

"Nothing. Meaningless scratches cover the last bit of marks, as if someone wanted to hide it."

Isabella grunted and leaped into the air. Hovering above them, she said, "Well, that's not much help. Sweetnettle's right. They wanted to go home but couldn't because they'd been turned into uprooters. I'm going to look around. Maybe I'll spot some." She flew off.

Enderfon stood. "It won't take me long either to reach the summit. I'll look down into the valley and see what's going on there."

The rock giant strode up the slope. Nnylf and Alana looked at each other and pulled down their caps. Sweetnettle flitted between them and Draako. He called out, "We can't stay here, especially if more uprooters are hiding nearby."

Alana nodded and searched Nnylf's face. "What do you think? Should we ask Isabella and Enderfon to come back? Draako is here. He can defend us."

It's not you who needs defending.

Alana cried out, "Isabella, where are you?" Her dragon dove toward her from the top of the sunsetside slope as the sound of Enderfon thudding down the opposite side of the mountain faded into the distance.

ENDERFON

WHEN HE REACHED THE slope's highest point, Enderfon scanned the coldside horizon. He saw nothing in the hot, dry desert valley below that crawled, flew, or burrowed. Everything looked calm.

A movement along the path between the slopes caught his eye. Two figures, one behind the other, were scurrying downhill. Close behind them, he could see a pack of furry beasts on the same path. They were hunting the first two and pointing to their fleeing prey. Isabella's shadow flickered overhead as she soared high above. She dipped her head twice; he knew she saw them, too.

Enderfon focused on the two fleeing figures. The one in front was a big buck goat. A man followed the goat, a young man with a familiar sack across his back, and—it was Kurnan! Enderfon slapped his forehead, which loosened a few embedded stones. Not only was it Kurnan, but he was in great danger. Uprooters were chasing him.

The giant knew his team of trackers must distract the uprooters before they tore Kurnan apart. He hurried down the slope back to his companions and found Isabella organizing everyone. She ordered Draako to kneel; Nnylf climbed up his foreleg to reach the rider's hump. Alana emerged from the cave with their bundles of supplies, which Isabella quickly thrust into her jaw pouch. Sweetnettle was hovering over Draako's head. When Enderfon returned to their campsite, the Lobli flew up to his shoulder and clung to his usual post.

"You saw them too, the uprooters?" Enderfon asked Isabella. She nodded, and he felt the poke of Isabella's thought probes. *Yes, they chase Kurnan and a buck goat, but why? Something strange about that goat.*

"Yes, very strange and they're not hiding from the Malevir."

The amulet will protect Kurnan.

Enderfon paused and rubbed his chin, which bristled with pebbles. He looked into Isabella's reddening eyes. "Those uprooters, they want the amulet for themselves."

ROCÁNONOM

THE ORB'S SILHOUETTE COVERED less than half of the sun. Dragonwolder would not have to wait much longer for a warmer World-Turn; but why now? Was the orb somehow tied to the Malevir?

Knowing he had much work to do, Rocánonom packed the few supplies he needed for his trek and left his tower. He could still see the little chary bird flying warmside. Her leg was carrying yet another of his messages, this one for Aurykk.

Silly of me to use the bird—Aurykk will know. But the bird might find him asleep. What if he frightens her? Rocánonom hurried down the scarp to reach a partly snow-covered path leading through the mountains.

He had no choice. Only one way remained to fight the Malevir and come to the trackers' aid. Rocánonom regretted endangering his old friend, but the Golden would understand the importance of his visit. How could he doubt his intentions?

If the trackers needed him again before he reached Aurykk, Rocánonom was sure Sweetnettle would find a way to tell him. Besides, the riders were safe. The combined powers of a rock giant's mace *and* two extraordinary dragons would protect them.

Anyway, why should he stay to watch the Coldside Sea Island tower? The Malevir was busy with Kurnan, wasn't he? Maybe he had left the island unguarded. Could the Malevir see any part of Dragonwolder whenever he wanted, or only places the amulet occupied? If the trackers retrieved the amulet, would the Malevir control them, too?

Preoccupied by all these worries, Rocánonom tripped over the rim of a hole opening up ahead of him on the path and nearly fell in. His supply kit slipped out of his hand, but he grabbed it before it fell into a dark, widening pit.

He sniffed and wrinkled his nose. Wet, dirty wool and filth—the stench of uprooters! Surely not here? He held his breath and peered into the pit. With one hand he gripped the rim's rough edge. With the other he summoned one of his small light-bearing orbs and directed it into the darkness. The orb illuminated a passageway. Figures he spied not far below nearly straightened his curly hair. A cluster of uprooters returned his gaze. Their opaque black eyes reflected his orb's light. He shivered at the sight of their matted, muddy fur and their long, curved claws, clotted with dirt and roots. Rocánonom looked in the direction of the digging and realized the beasts were tunneling into his mountain.

He needed a spell to stop them but not kill them. They were amnesic UrLoblin, his old friends, unaware they were trapped in a spell thrust on them so long ago by the Malevir. How to overcome that ancient magick with his own, with a spell powerful enough to turn them around and protect his tower?

Rocánonom pulled back from the hole, stood at his full height, and raised his arms to the sky. Only the Great Force of Water could help him now. His arms extended and fingers stretching toward the sky, he called out. His voice rang with an incantation that conjured roiling clouds into the sky overhead. Protected by the aura of his spell, he remained dry, but a cascade of hailstones battered the ground, chipping away at the hole's rim, and the uprooters retreated.

Rocánonom lifted his arms again and summoned rain. A few heavy drops spattered the ground, then a flood of rainwater filled the passageway. The uprooters would not drown. They would retreat into other tunnels that led away from his mountain. One last incantation froze the rain-filled hole. Dense ice plugged the passageway and seeped into the earth surrounding his mountain. No uprooters could dig through that frigid, impenetrable wall. Now he could resume his journey.

NNYLF

THIS ISN'T WORKING, NNYLF thought. He smiled at Alana and hoped she'd feel less contrary, but she paid no attention to his grin. Instead, she was arguing with Isabella. Fearing more harm would come to Kurnan if they grabbed him now, she refused to mount her dragon. "Come on, Alana. Those beasts will catch Kurnan and tear him apart. Hurry up."

He could see Alana's mouth set. "No, Nnylf, Kurnan will run away from us. The Malevir will hurt him if he thinks he's losing control over my brother. He might kill him."

Nnylf wanted to comfort her, but the dragons were impatient to leave. Isabella huffed billows of angry smoke, and Draako's flanks were twitching. "He's lost if we don't fly to him now. Believe me, we have no choice."

"We always have a choice," Alana muttered.

Enderfon called down to them. "The uprooters are close to him. The leader's claws are fully out and reaching for your brother. Shall we let the uprooters tear him apart?"

"Oh no, not that." Alana scrambled up Isabella's flank, settled into her seat, and held on as Isabella rose off the plateau and began her steep descent into the valley. "Let's go!" she cried out. "What are we waiting for?"

Nnylf leaned into his dragon's frill as he and Draako joined Isabella's steep dive toward the uprooters. The beasts surrounded Kurnan, and the leader's claws snapped at the young man's neck. Another uprooter tore at his cloak. Kurnan struggled to escape, but they pulled the torn cloak from his back.

Nnylf gagged as the leader pulled a long chain out of Kurnan's tunic. The leader grunted when he saw the amulet hanging from it. He yanked the chain from Kurnan's neck and palmed the amulet.

Isabella flew over the melee and opened her long jaws. Her forked tongue hung over her lower lip. She exhaled a cone-shaped cloud of gases, which settled over the uprooters and Kurnan and froze their movements. The lead uprooter's shaggy arm hung above his head like a curved tree limb, the amulet dangling from his claws. Kurnan, as motionless as his attackers, lay on the ground.

Nnylf realized Isabella must have released smaze, a gas that immobilized its target. Once the smaze vapors melted away, Nnylf slid off Draako's shoulder and ran toward the stunned creatures. He almost fainted from the uprooters' stench. He stretched and jumped to reach the pendant, which dangled high over his head in the uprooter's claws. Nnylf slapped at the amulet, and it fell onto Kurnan's chest.

Draako lowered his snout and would have given his rider a lift but, at that very moment, Kurnan jumped to his feet. He pushed Nnylf away from the uprooters. Nnylf somersaulted backward, the slope spinning around him as he fell. When he sat up and shook his head to clear his vision, he saw Kurnan slip the amulet's chain over his head. The buck goat materialized out of nowhere. Kurnan leaped onto its back.

The goat galloped down the slope and disappeared in a cloud of dust at the base of the mountain. *The Malevir sent that goat. Of course! To take Kurnan away from us.*

Nnylf wanted Draako to follow Kurnan down into the desert, but Alana, tears bathing her cheeks, begged the dragons to stay. Her voice, broken and muddled by sobs, pleaded with them. Her brother was alive. That's what mattered. They would find him, somehow, in the Coldside. Now perhaps they could free these uprooters too. Maybe *they* would help catch Kurnan.

With confused thoughts, Nnylf dabbed her face with his red cloth. "Here, my friend, let me dry those tears. You look like your grief will tear you in two."

Alana nodded her thanks and let him pat her face. She sighed and shrugged. "I don't think Kurnan knew me or Isabella. He ran from us—with the amulet. The Malevir controls him completely."

Nnylf's throat tightened as he dabbed at a new flow of tears. "Stop. Stop. You are right. When we help these beasts find their true selves again, we will make new friends. Let's try."

Alana sniffed and wiped her nose with her own red cloth. Then she hugged him. The warmth of her body suffused his own cloak, and for a few moments he thought of nothing more than holding onto this sweet and caring young woman. He wanted to protect her, but how could he do that and still help her rescue Kurnan? So many dangers lay ahead.

Alana pulled away from him and faced her dragon. "How did my brother escape your smaze? How soon will it weaken so we can free these poor beasts?"

"The amulet fell onto Kurnan and its magick revived him," Draako said. "The Malevir needs your brother for something—something dangerous I am sure. We must follow him."

"Alana, listen. Draako's right. We have to find out where he's going." Nnylf turned to the dragons. "Draako, Isabella, would you follow Kurnan without stopping him? To find out where the Malevir is taking him?"

Without a sound, the dragons spread their wings and headed for the dust cloud left by the galloping goat. Their thoughts remained with Nnylf and Alana. *The Malevir controls Kurnan, but cares nothing for the uprooters. While we are not here to guard you, do not leave Enderfon. He and Sweetnettle will guard you. Do not go near the uprooters. They won't move until we return.*

Then why can't we go closer to them? Alana asked.

Just. Stay. Away.

Nnylf watched the dragons soar over the desert until they disappeared behind the mountain. Alana's shoulders trembled when he pulled her close to his side to reassure her that he would protect her.

Alana pulled away from him and smiled slowly. "Don't be afraid, Nnylf, we'll be fine. I know we can save Kurnan and free him from the amulet's power." She lifted her chin and walked briskly toward Enderfon.

Slack-jawed, Nnylf stared after her.

PART 4

SHORT-LIVED PEACE

SWEETNETTLE

ISABELLA

SHE DIDN'T TELL DRAAKO, but he probably knew she had drawn a double dose of life forces into her Cone of Cold. Those uprooters wouldn't be going anywhere for a long time. Isabella looked back at the mountain slope before she and Draako flew above the wispy cloud layer that drifted over the desert.

Draako was calling her. *I can't see the goat because of that dust trail. More Malevir magick, isn't it?*

Most likely. Kurnan will need a place to hide, Draako. Where would he go? Oh, do you see that over there? It's a waterfall!

Yes, could be a good water supply and near a big hole in the rock wall. Give me a moment. I want to have a better look.

Me, too.

Isabella expanded her thin, vertical pupils, not to receive more light, but to magnify her vision by calling on primal energy that ran in her veins. She sensed Draako's vision expanding too. A small amount of energy helped them home in on their target.

That hole is the mouth of a cave, big enough for dragons.

For dragons? Do you suppose…? What was that? Do you see something or someone climbing up to it?

Isabella hovered above the clouds and closed her eyes until a surge of heat traveled down her long snout and up again, across the ridge that hung over her eyes. When the heat pressed against her lids, she opened her eyes again. Her heart jumped. The "someone" was Kurnan.

Isabella flew in figure eights as she sent Draako her finding. *We've found Kurnan.*

He sees us.

But the clouds…

Draako flew high above her. *If he saw us, then through Kurnan's eyes the Malevir knows we're here.* He rolled to his side, flipped his tail, and swooped back toward the mountain pass. *Look what's coming. Somehow, they revived before our return.*

Isabella could not contain the dark, angry blast of flames and smoke that forced its way out of her jaws. The heat grew at the sight of the uprooters they'd left immobile with Enderfon and the others. *How could they do this, Nnylf and Alana? We warned them. Draako, what if the uprooters attacked our riders? Wouldn't Enderfon protect them?*

I'm sure he would. This doesn't make sense.

We must go back.

First, let's see where these uprooters are going.

The two dragons hovered above scattered clouds and watched the cluster of shaggy beasts trudge along a rock-strewn path high above the entrance to the cave Kurnan had found. The leader, who had taken the Malevir's amulet earlier, was not among them. They looked like the same uprooters, but… The group stopped near a large boulder and rested. Some squatted and toyed with pebbles in the dirt, while others leaned against the boulder or sat on top of it.

Isabella and Draako followed their drifting cloud cover. Soon they dived into a patch of heavy gray rain clouds that had blown in from the mountaintop.

How long have we been watching them? The beasts aren't moving, and these clouds won't stay in one place. Isabella's concern for her rider grew as Alana failed to answer the thoughts Isabella was sending her. *I think we should leave them and return to our friends.*

Before Draako could answer her, the uprooters stood and gathered on one side of the boulder. Together, with their paws splayed against the rough stone, they heaved again and again until the boulder began to rock. Every time the uprooters pushed, the boulder tilted more until it teetered and rolled away from them. It crashed down the mountainside, heading directly for the ledge where Kurnan was standing.

ALANA

THE GROUND SHOOK UNDER Alana as Enderfon paced the path between the mountain slopes. Each step he took jarred her aching head. Her eyes itched with weariness, and she couldn't stifle her yawns. She rubbed her forehead, then looked down the path at the giant. He would protect her and Nnylf. No uprooter could challenge him and win.

The uprooters formed a frozen circle around their leader, his arm raised toward the sky. The Malevir's amulet no longer dangled from his paw. Nothing had changed here since the dragons flew off. *What could be delaying them, and why is there no message from Isabella?* Pangs of anxiety flooded her from head to toe, and her knees quivered. Her weak legs folded under her, and she dropped onto the path's rough, icy verge.

She looked up at a pair of booted legs. Nnylf was smiling down at her. He asked, "Why do you look so worried? Isabella and Draako will keep Kurnan safe, one way or another." He crouched beside her. "Anyway, I'd like to see you smile. I'd feel better knowing you were happy."

I know Nnylf means well, she thought, *but I wish he weren't so cheerful. How can he be sure our dragons will keep Kurnan safe? I can't stand all this waiting. What's wrong with me? I feel so dizzy. And where's Rocánonom and that magic codex of his? We need it to fight the Malevir. Oh, my poor brother. I don't know how we'll save you.*

Nnylf's fingers were tapping her fingers, splayed against the hard ground. She clenched her hands into fists and crossed her arms. "Nnylf, I'd smile if only I knew where Isabella or Rocánonom were right now."

"I am sure that the giant is doing all he can to help Kurnan, but you've heard nothing from Isabella?" He looked so intently at her that she was sure he was inspecting every freckle.

"No. Has Draako sent you his thoughts?"

Nnylf stood up, brushed ice crystals from the toes of his boots, and returned her gaze. "No, not a word. I don't understand."

A sudden, clammy sweat covered Alana's brow. She couldn't catch her breath. Her stomach churned, and spots bobbed between her and Nnylf when she looked up at him. Loud ringing masked his words. She barely heard him call her name before she lost consciousness.

When Alana opened her eyes again, she tried to move her weary arms and legs but gave up. Nnylf's face was close to hers. He was kissing her forehead and begging her to wake up. Nice, his kisses were nice. Soft. Damp. Quickly, however, her worries returned. "Nnylf, if our dragons don't call us, if we can't hear their thoughts, could they be…" She swallowed hard. "Could they be dead?"

Nnylf coaxed her to lie still. He covered her with his cloak.

"Don't do that. You'll freeze," she mumbled.

"You fainted. See how your worries hurt you? I promise, our dragons are careful and strong. When they come back, we'll move on from here. Please, rest a little while longer."

Alana's impatience surged. "How can I rest? How can you be so cool about this, Nnylf-Knows-It-All?"

Nnylf smiled and squeezed her shoulders. "You haven't called me that name since we were little." The thud of Enderfon's approach interrupted Nnylf's flirting.

"Riders!" he called to them. "I see your dragon friends returning from the desert."

Alana's heart leaped, and she had trouble breathing again. Relieved to know some horrible Malevir magick had not killed her Isabella, she grasped Nnylf's arm. He pulled her up, and she straightened her clothing. "Here, Nnylf, you'll need this," she whispered with a tight smile as she held out his cloak.

The young man caressed her cheek with a knuckle. "There, that's more like it. Let's wait for our dragons where it's warmer."

DRAAKO

W ITH ISABELLA HOVERING BY his side, Draako watched Kurnan disappear. "We've no choice. Back to our riders. Now." He thrust out his wings and soared upward. The force of Isabella's wingbeats matched his own.

They reached the pass. Draako looped over the mountain slope until he spied his party's camp. The scene below him was just as they had left it. How could the uprooters be here in the pass *and* there on the Coldside Desert cliff? Draako's bewilderment increased at the sight of Enderfon, waving his mace in greeting. Where were Nnylf and Alana?

Isabella's wings grazed his tail as they dived into the gap between the mountains. Locked in place were the beasts she had enchanted. Not one clump of fur had moved. He did not see Nnylf nearby.

"I don't know what to think. Which uprooters are these?" he asked Isabella.

"Those we left behind, or maybe others who ate our riders before attacking Kurnan." She moaned.

Draako belched a cinder ball and shook his head. "Don't say such a thing." He shot straight up then banked until he met Enderfon, who was striding up the path. Circling the giant, he asked after Nnylf.

Enderfon's laughter shook loose a few wobbly boulders. They rolled down the path. Draako blasted steam at them, and they swerved away from the uprooters.

"Alana will be relieved to see you again. She and Nnylf left me and the Lobli. They climbed the slope to find a safe place until you returned. Why did you not send your thoughts?"

"But we did! Why didn't Nnylf or Alana answer us?"

"Ah," Enderfon mused. "You tried too. This must be Malevir mischief. What of Kurnan?"

"We'll tell you all about what happened after I find Nnylf."

The dragons skimmed the slopes until they found their riders, who ran to greet them. Nnylf shouted "You're back. Thank the Ways of the World. When we didn't hear from you…" He hurried to Draako's side and patted his leg. "Tell me," he whispered, "did you find Kurnan?"

Alana ran to her own dragon and caressed her russet snout. "We didn't know if you were…"

"In danger?"

"Yes, well…" Alana leaned against Isabella's flank.

"I don't know, Alana," Draako said aloud. "Kurnan saw us."

Alana dropped her head and sighed. "Thank the Ways of the World. He's alive."

Draako added, "I'm sure the Malevir saw us through Kurnan's eyes. He knows we are tracking your brother."

"You see?" Nnylf frowned and pushed his fists into his hips. "I told you we'd never get at him safely. The Malevir's spells and tricks will always be in the way."

Draako snorted puffs of soot. "Uprooters are a bigger problem for Kurnan than the Malevir right now."

"Uprooters? They're spellbound and under our—your—control."

Isabella added, "These uprooters, yes."

"There are others?"

Draako's heart weighed heavily. He and Isabella nodded.

By now, Enderfon and Sweetnettle had climbed the slope. The sprite jumped off Enderfon's toe and ran to sit in Alana's lap. The rock giant stepped back a pace and squatted near them.

Draako began. "We followed Kurnan to a cave in a cliff jutting out from the mountainside. It has a view of the whole desert. Your brother's hair is dirty and his clothes are ragged. His tunic hangs on thin shoulders, but otherwise he looks lively."

Isabella spoke up. "The cave's mouth could swallow a dragon. We thought we'd look for clues—proof a dragon once lived there—but a band of uprooters surprised us. They loosened a boulder sitting above the cave."

"Imagine the sight. The boulder rolled downhill toward the cliff's edge. We were sure it would flatten Kurnan..."

Alana gasped and squeezed Nnylf's arm. He grimaced and pried open her tight fingers. She snatched back her hand. Reddening, she whispered an apology to Nnylf and rasped, "Please, go on, Draako."

"We wondered how the uprooters there could have escaped Isabella's Cone of Cold. Then we began to worry about you all, since your thoughts never answered ours. The uprooters pushed the boulder and disappeared into another small cave up the slope. The boulder bounced off the cliff and rolled into the desert. Fearing the worst, we looked for Kurnan. We caught a glimpse of him running into the big cave."

"Nothing more?"

"Nothing more. We tried to tell you, but I see our thoughts never reached you. So here we are."

"Yes, here you are," Nnylf said, "and your thoughts woke me moments ago. Why can I hear you now, but not when you were chasing Kurnan?"

Enderfon's voice rumbled across the mountain pass like distant thunder. "The Malevir cannot invade your thoughts as long as your dragons' primal energies are near you and protect you. Kurnan has no dragon Protector. The Malevir controls his mind."

Alana pressed her trembling fingers to her mouth. "But the beast *did* touch our minds. I could not hear Isabella."

Nnylf scooted over to her side and wrapped an arm around her shoulders.

Enderfon paused before answering her. Impatient, Draako turned to Enderfon and asked him to explain.

"True, Alana." The rock giant unfolded from his crouch and stretched. "Your every message turned to mist when your dragons neared the Malevir's magick. Now that Draako and Isabella are with you again, the beast's magick loses strength, but he still controls Kurnan."

A part of Draako welled up with anger as he remembered the uprooters' grunting and pushing before the boulder crashed on the cliff's edge and rolled away. He was sure his eyes were reddening with rage. "Yes, Kurnan saw Isabella but could not or would not listen when she called him."

"I would never abandon my rider. I just can't reach him," Isabella muttered, dark threads of smoke drifting up from her flaring nostrils. "I don't understand how the Malevir took control of his mind, why he shuts me out."

"He abandoned *you*," Draako replied and stared hard at Nnylf and Alana before adding, "We'll check on Kurnan every day. He won't stay in the shelter of the cave for long. The Malevir has other plans for him, I am sure."

Isabella added, "The day Kurnan abandons the cave, we'll follow him. By then Rocánonom and Aurykk will have given us a way to break the Malevir's hold on your brother."

"Meanwhile," said Draako, "we'll make camp here—after we free those uprooters." He pointed a claw at the spellbound creatures.

"How could I forget them?" Nnylf ran to the path for a glimpse and called back, "They haven't budged. Oh, Enderfon, my apologies. You can see them easily from there."

"Yes, I can, but the leader *has* started to move."

Draako wanted to keep his rider safe. There was only one way. "Everyone ready? We have to break that uprooter spell—now." Isabella nodded, and they leaped into the air to circle over the beasts. Nnylf and Alana were practicing the incantation they'd used to transform the ice pond's uprooters while Sweetnettle cleaned his wings and readied himself to greet more of his ancestors.

Standing near the still-unblinking band of beasts, Nnylf shouted, "We have no pond water to bathe them. How will the spell-breaker work here?"

Draako sent his thoughts to Nnylf. *We'll use melt water.* While circling their target, he shot flames at snow surrounding the uprooters. Puddles formed between the bumps and hollows on the slope nearby. Draako half closed his eyes; Aurykk's spell thrummed through his wings. *Isabella, are you with me?*

Ummmmn. My heart beats with yours.

Draako and his cousin looped around the beasts while, below them, Nnylf and Alana sang:

> Malevir done
> Rivelam undone
> Uprooters rebel
> To unravel the spell
> Your new life begun
> Rivelam farewell

Melted snow arose in a mist. It soon settled over the cluster of uprooters, masking them completely. Nnylf and Alana continued to chant until Draako and Isabella flew off to rest on a slope. Draako wearily glided to a dry, level spot. He was pleased to see the mist drift from the shivering beasts' bodies, which huddled around a drenched but frowning UrLobli. The creature's growl surprised Draako.

"What have you done to us?" screamed the sprite.

ROCÁNONOM

ALL IN ALL, THE journey had been easier since his baffling encounter with uprooters. Certain he had blocked their progress, Rocánonom continued his hike up a narrow mountain trail. He struggled from one challenging foothold to the next as here the path gave out and there it continued dry, above the snowfall.

The wind picked up. It wormed its chilling way through his cloak and tunic. Rocánonom considered calling upon the Great Forces one more time, to ease his crossing, but shook his head. *I shouldn't call them again, not so soon. Their power lies in the gravity of my summons. If I waste their benevolence on small matters of discomfort or annoyance, they will come less willingly to my aid.*

Rocánonom pulled his cap low on his forehead and tightened his cloak's waist cords. Ahead of him, but still a long way off, was Aurykk's mountain. He hiked alone on the trail, under a pale gray sky. No birds or other woodland creatures distracted him from the memories that surfaced each time he passed a familiar turn or landmark.

Nearing the ruins of Anonom, he remembered being there on a particularly alarming day many Moon-Risings ago. After the valley folk's final battle with the aiglonax, they had set about rebuilding Dragonwolder's villages and towns. Rocánonom, Sweetnettle, and four other Loblin went to Anonom to see what needed to be done there. The giant and his crew were inspecting rubble and wrecked buildings when icy winds began to buffet them with increasing force.

In the pale light of dawn, they looked up and noticed a dark orb in the sky. It blocked half the sun's light. "Do you recognize that shadow over the sun?" he asked his little friends.

When all but Sweetnettle shook their heads and began to shiver, Rocánonom advised them, "Perhaps it will move on. Anyway, we'd better speed up our work. A storm is brewing."

Sweetnettle piped up, "I think the orb brought these nasty winds. Is a Cold-Turn coming? I'm scared. What is that thing?"

Rocánonom was at a loss for an explanation. He suspected that the Malevir and the dark orb had a connection, but how? "Strange, it is," he said to the sprites. "If it does not move away from our sun, a Cold-Turn surely will begin and much too soon."

Sweetnettle added, "In my bones, I feel it is watching us." The other Loblin nodded and, in their small, chirrupy voices, let Rocánonom know they sensed a sad disruption in their future.

"Possibly, but enough of these notions and questioning. We must finish our work before the weather worsens."

Grumbling at the thought of a long, cold season ahead of them, the Loblin resumed their inspection without their natural bounce. They passed from one battered house to another and from broken-down shops to ramshackle stables, until they had enough information for a map.

While spreading a large piece of clean, cream-colored goatskin and preparing his inks, Rocánonom staggered when an unexpected gust scattered his writing materials and ripped the skin out of his hands. It sailed high into the air and out of sight over the Meeting of Mountains, where a vast storm was brewing.

He gathered the Loblin around him. A fierce downpour of sleet pounded them as they raced toward the largest manse in the village, standing in grand and desolate decay. He led his little band to its broad green door, which creaked open at his touch. They hurried inside.

Rocánonom was musing about that day, the first of a long Cold-Turn, when he came upon that old, familiar refuge, the same manse. Its door was ajar, as if someone had stepped out moments earlier. *Not nearly as forlorn-looking as I remembered it.* Curious, Rocánonom stepped inside. The door closed behind him.

ENDERFON

STANDING ON THE MOUNTAIN slope, Enderfon heard his dragon friends reassure the freed UrLoblin they were safe. He decided to stroll down the slope and join them. Warmed by the heated mist surrounding them, the ancient sprites were watching Sweetnettle work an incantation. The Lobli pointed to a pile of sky-blue, apple-red, coltsfoot-yellow, twig-brown, and moss-green garments he'd chanted from his bulging sack and trilled, "The UrLoblin seem happier now."

Nnylf and Alana sorted and passed out cloaks and other clothing to the UrLoblin, who thanked them and Sweetnettle. They began to dress themselves. Freed from the Malevir's cruel spell, they giggled as they wiggled into new brown leggings and pale shirts. Nnylf and Alana offered each of them a pair of boots, prompting another round of happy Loblin squeals.

When their leader sang out, "Oh, if only we had our tools and food pods again. How we've missed them," Sweetnettle patted his sack and sang a little tune. Soon the sack opened, five small packets rolled out, and the sack deflated.

Approaching the little band, Enderfon watched them untie each packet with their long, delicate fingers. They pressed their upturned noses to the cloth covering, sniffed and, lifting one flap at a time, opened the packets. Their cries of astonishment grew as they found new rucksacks. They pulled out sturdy twine, jars of ointment, and mittens, along with little hammers, chisels, and other tools every Lobli carries. At the bottom of the rucksacks, they discovered food pods and tiny chests filled with cakes and thick slices of bread spread with jam.

"Eat now," Enderfon said. "Nourish yourselves for our shared journey."

The leader of the five creatures looked up at him. "Halloooo, up there! You look like the giant in our old stories…like that Enderfon of the Warmside Beyond…oh, what were those stories about? Never mind, I am…oh dear, I've forgotten who I am." She looked down at her freshly shod feet and green speckled hands. "I suppose I am an UrLobli, but it's been so long. I remember very little of my life before the Malevir trapped us and…" She trembled and looked up at him again. "Please give me a name. Give each of us a name."

Feeling a great tug of sadness for the confused sprite, Enderfon crouched and murmured, "I remember UrLoblin who used to visit me at the red needlerock, when a spell bound me to the mountain crags. They swept away sharp, broken rocks and muck collecting in my body's crannies and clefts. They sang me sweet songs at sunsetting to lessen my loneliness. They offered me food, but I could no longer open my mouth. Before I fell into a long, deep sleep, their visits ended. Do you know those UrLoblin?"

Enderfon was sweating pebbles. His speech was too long. He guessed the UrLoblin were tired, but was surprised to see Sweetnettle in their midst, laughing with them, poking, and jostling. The leader waved to him and said, "Sweetnettle knows our names. I begin to remember too." She stepped closer to Enderfon. "We did find you by the needlerock, and we did care for you—until the Malevir captured us and made us his slaves."

Nnylf's voice was hoarse and rough. "His slaves? How? What kind of slaves?"

Each UrLobli took a turn to answer. "His spell turned us into uprooters. We were to dig his tunnels, all the way to the Coldside Desert."

"And make nesting places underearth."

"The basilisk nests."

"Monsters, those basilisks he sent to kill the dragons of Dragonwolder."

"He hates the dragon clans."

Enderfon interrupted them. "Do you know of other uprooters in the Veiled Valley?" Would his little group of trackers meet more of the shaggy beasts and stop again to break the spell that bound them? Surely, Kurnan would use that time to escape him and his friends.

Alana must have heard his thoughts. "Tell us, please, if other uprooters are out there. We follow my brother, Kurnan, caught in a terrible Malevir spell. Harm could come to all Dragonwolder if we don't stop him."

"How?"

"We think the Malevir wants to control Dragonwolder and all parts Beyond, so he is using my brother to carry out his plan."

Huddling shoulder to shoulder, the UrLoblin argued and shook their heads. They looked at Alana then turned back and resumed their discussion. One of them finally broke away from the group and raised one hand to make a visor over his eyes as he looked up at Enderfon. "Other uprooters, once our brothers, live near the Meeting of Mountains. They used to roam basilisk nests and pits down in the Coldside Desert."

Too many questions still bothered Enderfon. He placed his hands on his craggy knees. A loud crack filled the air as he straightened up. "Are they living there now?"

"We don't know."

With the sound of stone grinding against stone, Enderfon stood tall again. "We can't let Kurnan escape us. You know the tunnels, nests, and pits. Please help us catch him."

"Where is he now?" asked another of the five.

Isabella spoke up. "We last saw him enter the mouth of a huge cave, desertside."

The UrLoblin gasped as if they shared one breath. "The huge cave? We know it. A terrible place."

Enderfon whispered, "Will you go there with us? To save Kurnan and Dragonwolder?"

The sprites looked at each other and nodded to the one speaking for them. He took a few dainty steps toward Enderfon, looked at the dragons and their riders, then spoke to all of them. "We will join your journey." Sweetnettle ran to embrace them.

ALANA

AFTER HIKING FOR MANY days, Alana and her companions came to a bluff skirting the Coldside Desert. As she walked along its edge, she felt her spirits rise. Never taking her eyes off the trail, she lost herself in the rhythm of her boots, one following the other. Step. *We're getting closer.* Step. *We'll find him soon.*

She focused on better times spent with Kurnan, before havoc and devastation came to Fossarelick. They would play hide-and-seek games ending as soon as she opened their parents' cupboard and yelled, "Found you, ah-HA!" Kurnan would scream and scramble out of the cupboard, leaving a trail of clothing and linens on the floor. Mother, following the screams, would look at the mess and press her lips together, then burst into trills of laughter as she shook the pieces out, handed them to Alana and Kurnan, and told them to put everything back in the exact same order—or else.

Alana remembered evenings with family by the hearth. Father would tell them tales of Dragonwolder, of giants and dragons, of an enchanted island in the middle of the Coldside Sea, or of the mysterious Coldside Desert. Alana would sit back-to-back with her mother on a low bench. They'd knit, while little Kurnan snuggled into their father's ample lap. *Those weren't tall tales. Dragons, giants, monsters, and that island do exist. Now we're the so-called heroes of this story, but I don't feel much like a hero.*

The leader of the UrLoblin caught up with Alana. "Your dragons are resting nearby. We've shared a plan with them, the giant, and Sweetnettle. They all like it. Shall I share it with you?"

Alana looked at the cheerful creature, half her size. The color in her cheeks had blossomed into a healthy green, and a new orange scarf was wrapped around her neck.

"I like your scarf. Where did you find it?"

"Oh, would you like it? No? Well then." She paused. "I found it in my rucksack. Sweetnettle's a bit of a magician himself, I think."

"And he likes your plan? What is it?"

"Let me see, let me see. Oh, yes, Enderfon will keep you safe at the mouth of Kurnan's cave while we UrLoblin find your brother in the tunnels. Wherever he is, we'll find him because we know those tunnels like we know...like we know..." She pawed the air and scratched her ear.

"Like you know the back of your...hand?"

"Yes! That's it! How did you know? So, what do you think?"

"It sounds like a plan, but once you find him, what then?"

"Never mind. We'll take care of everything. Just wait for us outside the cave entrance until we come for you."

"Come for us?"

"Yes, to help us."

"I don't understand."

"You want to save Kurnan?"

"Yes, of course. I'll do anything."

"Then be patient and stay close to the entrance."

The UrLobli squeezed her arm and ran ahead to join the other UrLoblin. They scrambled down the path and out of sight. As they approached the once-distant cave from the other side of a jutting crag, the UrLoblin disappeared into the cave's mouth.

Alana turned to Nnylf, who was following her along the trail. "There they go." She studied his face. "How are you? It's been a long trek." Her heart beat faster as she waited for his reply. Somehow she was sure Nnylf understood her heartache, and her worries quieted for a while when he tried to cheer her up. Who else did that for her? Not even Isabella. But now he looked so tired. His new beard was sprouting in wisps along his jawline, and crescent shadows underlined his eyes.

"Weary, and you? But I think we're close now, thanks to those UrLoblin."

"Me too. Bone-tired, but I think you're right. The UrLoblin want us to wait until they come for us."

"I heard. With Enderfon watching, maybe we can rest."

Alana held onto Nnylf's arm as they hiked the last leg of their journey.

KURNAN

He liked his new home, a rock shelter facing the emptiness of the Coldside Desert. He'd left every person and dragon he'd ever known. He relished the silence of the desert's icy flats, stretching to the horizon. The voices had brought him to this nearly lifeless place, with no people and few creatures to trouble him, sunrising to sunsetting. Nothing to remind him of his broken life before the voices led him here. Except that nosy Silver Dragon who'd tried to kill him with a boulder. The voices had laid out the whole scene: a huge Silver had used its powerful breath to dislodge the rock. If Kurnan hadn't been wearing the amulet, he might have died. He should be grateful for the amulet. Thank the Ways of the World. Nothing more to worry about. The dragon had left. For good.

After those first dangerous moments, he'd entered the cave and looked around. It was bigger than that rock shelter up in the mountains. He unpacked his sack, his tools and weapons, set up a niche for sleeping, and built a fire pit. He felt a smile crease his face as he stepped back to survey his work—at last he was in his own world, far from the people and places that hurt so much.

The day after he found the cave, Kurnan explored his surroundings. He scrambled down the slope and soon noted easy prey: snow hares, black-footed mice, and a small wooly goat pawing the sparse sedge on the lowest slopes below his terrace. Patches of grass, nourished by melting ice, sprouted over the snow-covered slope. If he was quiet and fast enough, he could hunt and trap here every day. He would survive.

Kurnan thought about the times, before he rode a dragon, when he had been a happy boy living at home. His mother and older sister had taught him to build a hearth fire, clean his clothes, and cook a rabbit on the spit. When the fields didn't need attention, he and his father would hike—sunrising to sunsetting—through the forests of the Trace, the wooded hills between their village and the Coldside. Why did it all have to change?

Kurnan could see his father there, teaching him how to throw a dirk, use a bow, and fire arrows. To kill dragons, Father warned him, because they had turned against Fossarelick. Father joined other village men to hunt them until they were sure they'd killed them all; but the attacks went on. Their hunts continued for whatever beast might be preying on Fossarelick.

He remembered the day everything changed, when he was still a boy, the day the village emptied out. Some people went into the woods and meadows to forage for food. Father was with the other men somewhere in the mountains. Kurnan remembered being afraid; he hid in the cottage loft.

Nnylf's mother found him there and coaxed him out of hiding. She shared a secret with him: she was a dragonrider. She persuaded him to follow her to a meadow near the Trace where he met her dragon friends. One of them was Isabella. Kurnan became Isabella's rider, and together they hunted Aindle, the two-headed monster attacking Fossarelick's crops and animals. During a skirmish with Aindle, Kurnan lost his grip and slipped off Isabella's neck.

They were flying too close to the beast. Kurnan still could taste the aiglonax's bitter fumes. He stiffened at the memory of his limbs going numb and his sight clouding over. They said he nearly died.

After a few World-Turns, he knew his body had recovered, but confusion and anger muddled his thoughts. He disliked people talking to him. Their words jumbled in his head and lost all meaning. He wanted nothing more to do with dragons, especially Isabella. Kurnan didn't care that his sister replaced him as Isabella's dragonrider. He had no regrets.

Now the voices were his only company, not that he had invited them. Kurnan had wished they would fade away, but they'd stayed and they'd kept their promise. His head was free of pain. When he slept, however, nightmares would wake him to face morning bleary-eyed and shaking, his tunic and ragged breeches soggy with sweat. In the early cool part of the day, he staggered outside the cave and relieved himself in a gully. As the sun rose overhead, he rested under an overhang that shaded the rock shelter opening, and he worked on tasks: sharpening his knife blade and setting a goat trap.

A narrow stream trickled down the slope far from his waste gully. He would have plenty of water to drink. After another day, Kurnan yearned for better tasting water than the stream provided. Each sip smelled of rotten eggs. When he washed his hands in the stream, they didn't feel clean.

Dragons had fresh water running through *their* caves, or so he had heard. Maybe he would find sweet water in this cave. He liked the idea that, long ago, its wide entrance might have welcomed a yewr, a small group of dragons. It was wide enough for the biggest dragon he could imagine.

He instantly regretted thinking about dragons again, especially his former friend Isabella. When her great head swam through his thoughts, his stomach twisted, and he knew the sweats would start again. He ran inside. Cool shadows, well beyond the edge of the sunlight at the cave's opening, calmed him. He pressed the back of his head against a cold, smooth cave wall and prayed that the voices would leave him alone.

At the next sunrising, Kurnan decided to explore the cave's depths. He needed to carry a torch, but his fire pit was cold. How could he create a spark without the flints he'd lost while crossing the mountain pass? He paced across the terrace then remembered his father's lore about starting a fire. He spent half the day on the slopes searching for branches, twigs, dried leaves—anything that would burn.

When gusts of wind pushed at his back, Kurnan looked toward the far mountains. The last light of day was fading away, and he shivered in the growing chill. Gripping a thick stick and a broken branch he'd found, he re-entered the cave. He sat cross-legged on the ground and twirled the stick into the softer piece of wood until his arms ached. He was ready to put off the effort until the next day when wisps of smoke rose from the dead branch. Then a flame danced around the stick. He fed the flame dried grasses, and it grew big enough to relight the fire pit.

Reassured he could manage, Kurnan assembled a torch. He soaked strips of cloth in fat he'd saved to protect his face and hands from the harsh desert winds, then he tied the strips around the end of another forked branch he'd found on the slope. Packing enough grasses and fat to feed the torch, he set off to follow a passage leading from his shelter into the heart of the mountain.

Kurnan entered the dark recesses of the cave. He took a few hesitant steps into a passage far from the last light of day. Driven by his aching need for sweet water, he quickened his pace. The torch lit the winding path in front of him. Lime-crusted mounds, stalagmites, casting monstrous shadows across the floor, did not bother him until he heard loud buzzing, like the sound of Fossarelick bees foraging among wildflowers. He turned to look behind him. His foot caught the edge of a rut in the cave floor. His ankle twisted. He stumbled to his knees. He dropped his torch, and it bounced on the floor. Light and shadows playing on the cave walls broke into dazzling shards.

He closed his eyes and sat on the floor. His ankle ached. He realized the buzz was growing louder. The amulet in the hollow of his neck started to press into his skin. He wrapped his fist around it. It was warm. He squeezed it until his breathing calmed. The pain in his ankle eased. The buzz faded away. He opened his eyes and silently thanked the amulet again for protecting him. He guessed the voices favored his search for fresh water. When he could stand without shaking, he held the torch high and moved on under a towering stone ceiling.

More gouges and ruts broke up the gravel-covered floor as he walked deeper into the gloom. They made it harder for him to stay upright. He pressed his fingers against the rough wall to keep his balance. It was damp. From water? Had to be water. Certain now that he would find a fresh source just ahead, he hurried through the passage as it rounded a high curve. The cave floor sloped uphill and ended at a large opening in the wall. Torchlight revealed another passageway beyond it, but no stream or pool of water.

As Kurnan leaned into the opening, a harrowing chill enveloped him. The buzzing sound returned, now from somewhere deep in that dark space. It sounded less like bees now and more like someone muttering. The amulet pulsed against his throat then rested quietly. He shook his head. Dark silence returned, except for his gurgling hunger pangs. He ignored both. The bottom edge of the opening was even with Kurnan's waist. He climbed through the opening, one leg at a time, over its rough, crumbling edge.

He stood, awestruck. Ahead of him lay a broad white wall streaked with black and gray lines—like a frozen waterfall enchanted into stone. Hollow tubes pierced the stone wall. They were high and wide enough for him to walk through. He did.

༄

Kurnan's legs trembled with weariness, as if he were trekking again across the Veiled Valley, from one end of the mountain chain to the other. The tube widened as he went forward. Its curved walls fanned into a space too big to see by the light of his torch. He reached the far end of that vast space and sighed—deep grooves also cut across this floor. The path ended at another wall, where a high pile of boulders rose to block another passage beyond. Kurnan could see an opening toward the top of the pile.

When his eyes became accustomed to the gloom, Kurnan looked around the enormous chamber. The pile of boulders threw shadows onto the cave floor. Something other than his weak torch was lighting the boulders from behind; but the half-light filling this space came from somewhere else.

He looked up. Directly overhead and far above him hung a solid circle of ice embedded in the chamber's ceiling. Beams of soft light, filtered through blue-green ice crystals, were interrupted by the boulders' long shadows, and pale light settled throughout the chamber.

Where he stood gazing up at the ice, the air was damp—*there must be water nearby.* An odd musty smell enveloped him, like the mucky stink of his boots after trudging through the muddy fields where his family's oxen grazed. He pointed the torch toward the base of the boulders. White sand covered the floor. Then he noticed something else. Long, sand-filled furrows led into the pile of boulders.

Kurnan rested on one knee and let sand run through his fingers. It was moist. He gripped a slippery rock to stand. His hand slid off the rock, and he stumbled into a narrow stream he had missed in the gloom. Now he noticed, dripping down the pile of boulders, little rivulets of water feeding the stream. He followed its course until he came to the edge of a pool. He barely missed tumbling into it—level with the floor, the water was almost invisible.

Kneeling again, Kurnan dipped a small pot into the pool. One sniff gave him all the information he needed—he had found a supply of sweet water and lots of it. He gulped one potful after another. It tasted like mountain ice. He drank until his belly ached. After sticking his torch firmly into the sand, he sat cross-legged at the pool's edge and puzzled over a way to carry this water back to his shelter.

A wave of regret washed over Kurnan. What was he doing here, in this strange and unfriendly place? Although plenty of sweet, fresh water flowed here, he had no way to bring it back to his shelter, and he had no wish to remain here, without food or a warm fire pit.

The amulet was pulsing against his neck. Then that annoying buzzing returned, becoming louder. His torchlight bounced off the water-slicked wall, shivered, and flared wildly. The light broke into millions of flashing diamonds, in changing and dissolving patterns, and he fell to his side. As he lay on the floor, pulling at the amulet, he could hardly breathe. He stopped struggling when he heard a small, cold voice.

"Aindle, is that you?"

It was an echoing voice, not in Kurnan's head. He squeezed his eyes shut, groaned, and rolled back and forth in the sand. Why here? Would the voices start haunting him again? What did they want of him?

When he opened his eyes, he was in total darkness. It had to be after sunsetting. The amulet was burning his skin. He yanked it out of his tunic but could not break its cord, growing tighter around his neck. The amulet glowed and cast a soft light. Kurnan stood up. The cord loosened, and he could distance the disk from his body. He directed its small light toward the floor near his feet, which walked against his will toward the pile of boulders. His torch leaned toward the pool, its flame dead.

ROCÁNONOM

THE DOOR CLOSED BEHIND him and faded away. Rocánonom smiled then shook his head. "It was a good spell then and it works now," he whispered. He looked for the stairway. "Ah, there you are, my friends." Four sprites jostled each other up high, wide steps until they reached the giant. They pulled on Rocánonom's leggings and hurried him down the stairs, under a vaulted ceiling, into the rooms below.

As if expecting his arrival, the Loblin led him to a table set with bowls of berries, roasted acorn patties, and platters of breads and cakes. Two of them vanished behind a curtain then returned with a tray bearing plates, goblets, and spoons. Giggling among themselves, they bowed as they pointed first to the dishes and then to their little mouths, glistening with small white teeth.

Rocánonom joined in their game. He sat in a huge, comfortable chair, picked up a honeyed barley cake, and offered it to a red-haired Lobli whose bouncy curls would not stay under his loose green cap. The sprite giggled, turned deep green, and scurried behind the curtain. A second sprite, in leather leggings and a brown vest woven from meadow grasses, pointed to the dishes before climbing onto

Rocánonom's lap and slipping a cake into his mouth. Coughing out crumbs and laughing, Rocánonom wiped tears from his eyes and smiled. "My dear, dear old friends. How happy I am to see you again."

The tallest of the four Loblin bowed and nibbled on a handful of berries. "We have kept the hearth warm, polished the chairs and tables, preserved the fruits and grains, swept away the cobwebs, and given the field mice their own warm corner, but we haven't served you in a very, very, very long time." He frowned and sniffed a chunk of dark bread before popping it into his own mouth.

The curly-haired Lobli thrust the curtain behind himself and tiptoed up to Rocánonom's knee. "It's true. We've had no one to serve, ever since the dragons called everyone away to fight the...the..." He hesitated and blushed again.

"The Malevir?"

The four Loblin covered their eyes then nodded in unison. They gave him a searching look, which told him how little they knew about the Veiled Valley's recent past.

"The valley's folk and their allies, dragons living or ghostly, battled the Malevir's horrible aiglonax, and they destroyed it. The monster that destroyed this village and menaced Dragonwolder is no more," Rocánonom said.

The Loblin hugged each other, joined hands, and danced in a circle. Bumping into each other, they tumbled to the floor and giggled until Rocánonom sobered them with his worries about the Malevir's return.

The tallest Lobli helped his three brothers to stand; then, with an unsmiling face, he turned to Rocánonom. "We must remain hidden, I fear. If the Malevir finds us, he'll turn us into goblins as he did to other Loblin."

"That's unlikely now, yet..." Rocánonom muttered.

"Still and all, we hope someday to travel at your side again. For now, stay the night and rest before the next part of your journey."

"I thank you, but I should move on. Your kindness and hard work here have helped so many, including me. Guard this house until Anonom's people return to rebuild their town. Meanwhile, open your door to my friends if they knock in times of trouble."

Two Loblin leaned on Rocánonom's legs. Each sprite wore a leafy cap and sported a little braided beard. Hugging his knees, they began to sing a soft lullaby slightly out of tune with each other. Rocánonom opened his mouth wide to yawn. Soon his head slumped and the room filled with loud snores. With a chortle, the taller Lobli tossed a few berries in and the giant coughed, chewed, and wiped his mouth.

"Yes, perhaps I should rest here for the night, but—"

"No 'buts,' please." The curly-haired Lobli offered him a basin of warm water and a rough stone to rub his hands clean. Rocánonom thanked him and, after drying his hands, he followed the sprites to another large chamber. Against the wall was a bed, long and wide enough for four people. Soft canvas mattresses filled with straw were piled high on its rope bedstead, and a coverlet lay folded at the foot of the bed.

A small hearth, built into the opposite wall, bathed the chamber in a red-orange light that soothed the weary giant. He waved to the Loblin, already whisking themselves away behind a dark curtain that separated the guest chamber from the main room. Having folded his cape and pulled off his boots, Rocánonom loosened his tunic and crawled onto the stack of mattresses. He sank into them and closed his eyes.

As he fell into the welcoming coziness of the great bed, he began to dream. He saw himself in Aurykk's lair, trapped in a long passageway leading to the Golden's nest. Beyond the mouth of the cave, he saw a pair of enormous rocs carrying Aurykk away. Rocánonom could not move; in the dream, his legs were glued to the floor. The rocs dropped Aurykk into the Coldside Sea. Soon Rocánonom saw himself floating over the sea. He dragged Aurykk's dead body over the waves and toward the rocks guarding the Coldside Sea Island's shore. He heard someone scream, "He's gone!" Rocánonom woke up, and his eyes snapped open.

How could he have let himself slip into the comfort of that meal and this bed? *Aurykk is in danger. He needs my help.*

He jumped off the pile of mattresses, dressed, secured his cape and supplies, and hurried into the main chamber. The curtain was gone. Where were the Loblin? The hearth was dead. No trace of food or dishes remained on the now dusty and cobwebbed table and chairs.

Of course. He sighed. *They knew I would leave. No one must know I stopped by. No one will know my Loblin guard this place—unless they are needed.*

KURNAN

A NEW SILVERY-GREEN LIGHT BATHED the furrows leading to the heap of boulders. Despite Kurnan's resistance, his feet pulled him toward the boulders and the passage they blocked. A new voice, buzzing like an insect trapped deep in his head, urged him on. It grew louder as he moved forward. That sound, he knew it well. He'd heard it before, when he was wandering through the tunnels.

The buzzing became a dull, wordless throbbing; it rattled his ears at first. His chest hurt as he coughed and wheezed in rapid, shallow breaths. The closer he came to the boulders, the louder the throbbing. Kurnan stopped and pressed his hands to his head. He tried to squeeze out the noise.

The chilling voice called again. *Aindle, is that you?*

"No," Kurnan answered, lips trembling. "Aindle is dead."

Aindle, you've come at last. I forgive you.

Kurnan wrapped his arms around his shoulders and rocked from side to side. *Someone is on the other side of the boulders. Someone—or something—is casting that silvery-green light.* He shook his head and looked at the furrows. *Did that* something *make those ruts in the cave floor? How big is it?* Too frightened to move, he stared at the light.

His old, familiar voices shook him out of his trance. *Answer him. Say you have come for him.*

His mouth felt like the cracked mud of a dry river bed. Kurnan swallowed hard and licked his lips. "I have come for you."

Yesssss. We shall be together again. Kurnan's heart nearly froze.

"Again?"

My powers increase with your every word.

"What powers?"

Before the answer came, a heavy blow to his chest knocked Kurnan to the floor. In the dim light, he could not see what held him down. He could feel hands pushing his arms, legs, and head against the floor. He saw the silhouette of a small creature against the light pouring more brightly between the boulders—a person half his size. His head jerked up as that person yanked at the cord around his neck. *The amulet. They're taking the amulet.*

Dazed, Kurnan called out, "You mustn't take it! The voices—the pain...ahhh!" He groaned. The creature looked at the amulet, spat on it, and dropped it on Kurnan's chest. His attackers rushed about, binding his arms and legs behind his back. He couldn't move and his shoulders ached.

As he lay on the cave floor, damp grains of sand dug into Kurnan's cheek. The creatures planted his torch next to him and wrapped the loose ends of the cord around it. He begged them to untie him and let him return to his cave, but they answered with tinkling laughter and ran into the passageway he'd used, not long ago, on his search for water. Only his head could move, but the sand scratched his skin, and he thought it best to lie still for a while—until he heard distant rumbling.

Light filtered through the crystalline window overhead. With a new day coming, Kurnan hoped he'd think of some way to undo the cords. His thoughts evaporated as the rumbling became a roar. He looked up. The faint light revealed another feature of the chamber, a long set of steps leading from a shadowy corner near the crystal circle down to the floor.

Kurnan stopped breathing. His limbs tightened with fear. Cold sweat soaked his tunic. The beasts who had chased him on the mountain slope were descending the steps. Their acrid odor washed over him moments before they surrounded him.

He wanted to scream but he'd lost all control. He couldn't find his voice as the uprooters tore at his soiled clothes. *Rivelam...die, fie*—he could not remember the voices' spell. *Uprooters. Fie and die,* he croaked. One of the shaggy beasts grunted when it spied the amulet stuck to Kurnan's sweaty chest. Its long claws reached for his neck, and he closed his eyes, sure he was about to die. The uprooter tore the amulet from its cord and, with a jubilant roar, held it high in the air.

At the sound of a tremendous crash, Kurnan's ears filled with sharp pain. He twisted his body and saw the boulders in a heap on the floor. The chamber was filled with eerie light. Kurnan cringed at the sight of a gigantic beast, spikes running along its back. The cave floor shuddered as the beast thudded in his direction.

Only the muffled sound of scattering uprooters reached his ears, but he heard the beast's thoughts: *Aindle, they are hurting you.*

Kurnan's voice failed him.

I will save you, as always. With those words, the beast opened his mouth wide, and a long forked tongue lolled over his lower fangs. Kurnan laughed when he recognized this huge creature. He realized he, of all people, was about to be eaten by a Golden Dragon.

But he wasn't the dragon's target. Like a long rope of red lightning, the dragon's fiery breath swept over the uprooters and pulled them into a tight bunch. Their fur crackled as flames raced over their bodies. Kurnan was grateful his headache dulled their screams. He rolled his face into the sand. They were horrible creatures, but he pitied them. *I'm next.*

Aindle, I saved you—again.

Kurnan's arms and legs relaxed as the cords loosened. Unsure of the dragon's intentions, he lay stone still.

Stand up.

"I can't."

You can.

Kurnan, ready to dodge any sudden dragon move, pushed himself slowly from the cave floor, stood up, and brushed sand from his leggings. "Good?"

Good.

He pulled on his torn, sticky tunic and looked at the remains of his attackers. A pile of charred, delicate bones stood between him and the dragon, bones too small to carry the uprooters' bodies. Puzzled, Kurnan crouched near the ashes and skeletons for a closer look.

A glimmer caught his eye. The amulet. He snatched it from the mess and brushed off the ashes clinging to its face.

Kurnan, make a new cord, firm voices commanded him.

His voices! Where had they been when he'd needed them moments ago? He searched the floor for the cords that had bound his arms and legs and found a long, slender piece. No sooner had he slipped the amulet over his head than the dragon spoke to him.

Aindle.

No, I'm Kurnan.

You are Aindle. I am Lustredust.

The floor seemed to sway. *They said you were dead.*

We must leave. Hurry. You will ride me.

Kurnan crossed his arms. *I don't ride dragons.*

Ride me or die.

His voices were silent. The Golden lowered his neck and waited. Willing his feet forward, Kurnan drew near the dragon's snout. He knew the dragon's eyes would show his mood—dangerous or accepting. He looked at the great eyes staring at him. No color filled them.

No red for rage, green for curiosity, nor amber for contentment. White, his eyes were white.

Aindle, we are friends.

"My name is Kurnan."

Aindle, my rider, we must fly.

Kurnan stared into the Golden's colorless eyes. He hadn't expected to feel such heaviness in his limbs. A strange dullness fogged his thoughts. "What…what…should I…do?"

Take your place behind my frill.

I have no choice. I ride the dragon, or he will turn me into cinders, like those beasts. He hesitated for a moment, then he gripped the small spines along the Golden's front leg and climbed until he reached the hump behind the dragon's neck frill. Memories of sitting on Isabella's hump flooded his thoughts, and his empty stomach churned. He wanted to vomit; bile burned his throat. *Voices, where are you?*

Silence answered him. The great beast crouched low and sprang toward the ceiling of the chamber, straight at the crystal circle. Kurnan's neck snapped back. He squeezed his eyes shut and grabbed Lustredust's frill with the scrap of strength left to him.

As the dragon flew higher, Kurnan peeked through his lashes. He saw daylight streaming through layers of ice. Lustredust was hovering below the dazzling, faceted disk. The dragon loosened his jaw and released a cloud of steaming dry ice pellets. They pierced the ice, and a gas cloud hid everything in the chamber, including the charred uprooters. Lustredust shot through the cloud and out of the hole.

Humming filled Kurnan's ears.

Bzzz. We are free.

Were you calling me to you, Lustredust? With that buzzing I heard in the passages?

Surely, Aindle, you knew I was waiting for you.

Me? But I'm Kurnan. Where are you taking me?

You are *Aindle. We go to the Cave of Refuge, and then...*
And then...
To the Master.

PART 5

ELEMENTALS

ROCÁNONOM

THE AIR WAS SO still that Rocánonom imagined the whole of Dragonwolder sat silent. Under a canopy of gray sky, he summoned the wind and waited. Nothing happened—not even a gentle breeze brushed his cheeks.

At a sudden clap of thunder, the giant's breath caught in his throat. A mass of dark, roiling clouds took shape and hung sullenly overhead. Recovering from his surprise, Rocánonom whispered a short enchantment. The clouds lined up like a colossal string of gray puffballs. With a wave of his hand, he set them spinning until a steady wind blew from the center of the cloud wheel. Rocánonom turned his back to it and returned to the trail, and the wind thrust him forward while bending every tree along the route.

The success of his spell reassured Rocánonom. He hoped the wind would push him quickly toward the Sunsetside Mountains, to the Orferan dragons' Cave of Refuge. Pointing his finger toward Aurykk's mountain, he commanded an even stronger tailwind. He assumed the spell would build until he reached the mountain base.

Rocánonom smiled as the lower slopes of Aurykk's mountain came into view. *No magician giant has ever held such power. First, the*

Water Elemental did my bidding, and now the Air Elemental is my ally. When I have my hands on that grimoire, I will have all the knowledge I need to fight the Malevir. He chuckled and adjusted his pack, loosened by gusts of wind straining to pull it from his shoulders. He tightened his cap and strode ahead.

All at once, the powerful wind dropped. Rocánonom heard a low growl, as if the mountains themselves were gnashing their peaks together. He turned to see the wheel of clouds spin ever faster until it became a roaring vortex. The spiraling funnel danced toward him. Rocánonom searched the trailside for shelter. Finding none, he stood as tall as he could and shouted, "Great Elemental, Air Supreme, do you attack me?"

The vortex stretched at both ends and twisted itself into the shape of a ghostly gray dragon. The creature's body filled the sky.

Who are you to ask? You are not my master.

Rocánonom's words would not form in his dry mouth. Barely a squeak escaped his lips. Better to address this spirit in silence. He sent his thoughts: *Can you hear me?*

I hear you.

I beg your forgiveness. I command no one. I only ask for help. A strong sulfurous smell filled the air. The Elemental dragon writhed and dived toward him.

Veering away from Rocánonom, the creature split into two versions of himself, then into four. They came at Rocánonom from all sides. The ground fell away from him as they lifted him high above the trail.

Magician, you toy with our energy. Elementals are the power sustaining Dragonwolder and are not to be wasted in foolish play.

Air Supreme, I do not play. My journey must end with the Malevir's defeat, for even now he attacks Dragonwolder.

We care little for that.

Rocánonom pleaded his case. *You care little for Dragonwolder?*

We care little about your journey.

I called on you because the Malevir intends to destroy our world unless I find a way to stop him. My weapon against him lies hidden in the Orferans' Cave of Refuge. Please help me reach the cave soon.

Why? You offended us.

Each Air Elemental's eyes glowed red. Rocánonom searched his memory for a spell to cushion his fall since he expected them to drop him to the ground.

I meant no offense.

You regret your foolishness?

I surely do.

You will respect and protect the Orferans?

If you permit me to do so.

Then perhaps your cause is just.

You'll help me?

The wraiths did not answer. Frigid gusts jostled Rocánonom and tore at his cape. He was grateful for his thick cap. He looked below, hoping to discover where the dragon spirits were taking him. The roofs of Fossarelick rose out of the valley mists. The spirits hovered over the village. In an instant, he found himself in the middle of a Fossarelick barley field. The Elemental quartet was gone.

Plucking dried barley stalks from his cape and his chestnut curls, Rocánonom nodded as Kurnan's parents, Kirrill and Sherca, repeated their questions.

"Yes, yes, Kurnan is alive, and Alana, too. She and her dragon visited me in my tower before they left to track Kurnan, toward the Coldside Desert."

"How can she be safe if she is following him into the Coldside? That's a terrible idea." Sherca looked at him with pleading, tired eyes. Her son's troubles had aged her.

"I know, but—"

"No, Rocánonom. You don't understand. Just coldside of the Meeting of Mountains, Lustredust disappeared so long ago. The dragons say the Malevir killed him."

Seerlana added, "That's when the friendship with our dragons began to die."

Those words sent a chill through Rocánonom. Rising from his seat, he paced before the hearth and fought the panic threatening to close his throat. *I'd forgotten. That place is haunted by angry dragon spirits. I must get to the Cave of Refuge. No time to waste.*

To calm Kurnan's parents, he said, "Isabella protects Alana. You know the Copper loves her, even while saving a place in her heart for Kurnan." He turned to Nnylf's parents and his sister Azile. "Nnylf and Draako journey with them. As do two other Dragonwolder friends. My messengers tell me they are well and unharmed."

Eunan, Nnylf's father, said, "Your news will gladden all of Fossarelick." He pointed to Kurnan's family. "My friend here, Kirrill, wants to find his son, as do I, but our legs are not as strong as they once were, and we have no dragons to carry us hence." He tightened his arm around his wife's shoulders. "Seerlana's dragon will not wake until the end of the Cold-Turn. Who are these new friends of Dragonwolder who take such a risk? Do they ride dragons yet unknown to us?"

"I will explain everything to you. Many pardons for not telling you sooner, but I cannot tarry long."

Seerlana, once a strong and sinewy dragonrider, now leaned on Eunan as the families drew closer to Rocánonom in the great hall of Fossarelick. Unlike Kurnan, Seerlana's recovery from the Malevir's attack was incomplete. The aiglonax's poison had paralyzed one of her legs, and her hair, once a glowing auburn, had turned as white as the ice fields across the Veiled Valley.

"I would have forced my dragon from her deep sleep if I thought I could rescue our children, but you see I must leave that task to others now." Seerlana's eyes closed, and she sighed as she leaned into Eunan's embrace.

Azile hastened to bring her mother a cushioned bench, where they sat side-by-side. Rocánonom noticed how well she had matured into a tall, strong adult.

Kurnan's parents sat glumly on three-legged stools. Kirrill spoke up. "Our hearth is warm, but your tea will grow cold. Drink up and explain things to us, as you promised." Sherca coughed and he added, "Please," and folded his arms across his chest.

Other villagers straggled into the hall to share a midday meal and gawked at the handsome giant. Rocánonom nodded to them then turned to the dragonriders' families. He told them as much as he knew about the path their children had taken. He thought they must be feeling a mixture of relief and worry. When Rocánonom described Enderfon and Sweetnettle, everyone gasped. Now they knew Enderfon really existed and the legend of the three giants was more than a hearthside story.

Seerlana placed her hands on Azile's shoulder and stood up. "Such mixed blessings. Our children are alive. They face great danger and meet it bravely. Poor Kurnan, so unhappy and confused. Dear giant, thank you for easing our minds, as much as you could. Won't you stay and rest the night?"

I can't stay, not with thoughts of Lustredust eating away at me. "If I do not leave you right now and continue my journey, I will be too late to help your children. The Malevir is stronger than ever and I must go where I can reclaim the source of power we need to succeed."

The villagers did not question Rocánonom further. Offering him food, warm wraps, and water for the road, they gathered close to him and wished him a safe journey. Calling on the Ways of the World to bless them, Rocánonom offered his thanks and left the great hall. *They must never know the strength of the Malevir's hold on Kurnan.*

That is my secret—and Alana's. Oh, Ways of the World, oh, Great Ele-mentals, do not fail me now.

No wind blew him along his path. The air was still. Even the blackbirds had ceased their calls. Daylight was dimming. Rocánonom quickened his pace as he made his way once more toward the Cave of Refuge.

NNYLF

AFTER THEIR FIRST NIGHT spent sleeping outside the cave, Nnylf urged Alana to come in out of the cold. He suspected they'd have to stay at least another night until the UrLoblin's return.

"It's so dark and gloomy. Who knows what else is in there?"

"The UrLoblin would have made a lot of noise if something attacked them. Look, you don't have to agree right now, but I think we'll freeze if we don't shelter from the wind tonight."

"I'm warm enough now." She turned her back.

Nnylf released his breath with a hiss. "Alana, let's go in. Enderfon's watching us. We'll look around, make sure it's safe. If you…"

"If I don't like it?"

"We'll stay out here tonight."

Alana nodded but, before they entered the mouth of the cave, Nnylf noticed she was hugging herself and staring at her boots. He didn't like the cave much himself. Before Alana woke up, he'd peeked inside and shivered at the sight of its damp, sticky walls and endless dark depths. What was it like for Kurnan? Why had he left? Alana must be so worried. "You're afraid of what you'll see in there, aren't you? You know, I am, too, a little bit."

She nodded again. "Kurnan's been here. I don't know what he's been doing."

Nnylf flicked at the ashes sitting in a rough hearth by the entrance. "He had a fire. Look, rabbit bones. At least he was eating."

In a niche against the cave wall lay what must have been Kurnan's bedding. "That's my brother's blue coverlet." Alana's voice was caught in a sob as she ran to the niche. "He brought it from home, Nnylf. He must have cared enough about us to take it with him."

Nnylf rubbed his arms. *I doubt it. He probably took whatever was handy.* "It's cold in here, Alana. Maybe Kurnan knew where he was going, that he'd need warm covers."

"Or the Malevir knew."

"Don't say the beast's name," he rasped. "Who knows if he can hear us? Wait, what's that?"

"What?"

"I hear footsteps. They're coming from there." He pointed to a dark passage in the cave's recesses.

"Let's get out of here!" Alana tugged his sleeve. "Enderfon! Enderfon!"

෧

Nnylf wished the five UrLoblin would stop talking all at once. He couldn't understand anything for all the squeaks and coughs that came rushing out of their mouths. Running his hands through his hair, he looked at Alana and rolled his eyes. She tilted her head and shrugged. Nnylf mouthed, "Please, help me calm them."

Alana winked and held out her arms. She beckoned the UrLoblin closer and squatted in front of them. "Please, take turns and tell us— very slowly— what happened in there."

One of the UrLoblin elbowed through the others. Looking embarrassed and breathing hard, she called Sweetnettle to her side and whispered in his ear. The Lobli nodded and, clearing his throat, spoke for her. Nnylf leaned down closer to listen.

"Nnylf, Alana, and Enderfon, my brothers and sisters ran as fast as they could, but they have little good news for you. They scouted all the underground passages here. They know them so well, but new ones marked by uprooter claws surprised them."

"We did find Kurnan in a big chamber," piped up the short UrLobli, her cheeks mottled by dark green patches.

"Deep inside the mountain," said another UrLobli.

"We caught Kurnan and tied him up for you," gushed a fourth sprite.

"Where is he?" Alana cried out as she moved to search the depths of the cave entrance.

"He escaped."

Nnylf could not imagine where Kurnan could go without meeting him and Alana. "Did he run into other passages, deeper in the mountain?"

The UrLoblin looked at each other, then at the ground. "No."

Sweetnettle explained, "After tying up Kurnan, they left him and turned back to find us. The sound of roaring and gnashing stopped them." He wiped away some tears. "When they followed the sounds to their source, they found bones on the floor. Brittle bones, licked by flames."

Alana gasped. "Human bones? Kurnan's?"

The shortest UrLobli answered, "No, bones of *our* brothers. Flames released them from the Malevir's uprooter spell."

Nnylf's stomach churned. "That's horrible. If the bones weren't Kurnan's, where did he go?"

"Up."

Alana hiccupped a nervous giggle. "Up? In the air? He can't fly."

The UrLobli blushed a deep green. "No," she squeaked. "He flew through the big chamber's roof on the back of a dragon."

Nnylf found himself frozen, staring in disbelief. "A dragon?"

"Yes, a Golden. He scorched our wretched, ensorcelled brothers then flew through the roof of the chamber toward the Sunsetside Mountains."

Nnylf turned to Alana. "Aurykk? Could he have been here?"

She shrugged. "How? He's old and sleepy. And he would not have burned uprooters."

Nnylf wondered why Sweetnettle was pacing. The Lobli stopped, scuffed the gravel-covered cave floor, then slapped his forehead and looked at Nnylf. "The only other Golden in Dragonwolder was Lust-redust, but he's dead."

No, Sweetnettle, he lives. The Malevir brought him back to life. We saw him leave here. As she said, he flies sunsetside.

Nnylf jumped as Draako's voice echoed in his head. "Why?"

To wherever the Malevir leads him, but I do not know why. Come. We must follow. Bid the UrLoblin farewell.

Nnylf thanked the sprites for their help. They exchanged worried glances. "If you no longer need us, we will bury our brothers' remains, then go home."

"Home?"

"Back to the underearth for now. Farewell." With hardly a glance behind them, the UrLoblin re-entered the cave.

Nnylf waved goodbye then turned again to Draako. "Won't Lustredust attack us if we follow him?"

Draako did not answer. The Silver skidded onto the ledge, and Isabella soon followed.

Come.

Arguments would be useless. Nnylf mounted and waved to Enderfon and the Loblin. Draako's commands rang in his ears: "Rock giant, you and Sweetnettle will follow us on the ground. You will hear us when we call for you. Until then, watch out. The Malevir will try to mislead you."

The rock giant boomed, "The Malevir's plan tightens. Don't let your love for Kurnan blind *you*," but the dragons were soaring into the clouds, too far away to hear the warning.

KURNAN

As if he were sailing into a tempest at sea, Kurnan dodged frigid fingers of wind clawing his cheeks. He bent into Lustredust's neck frill and clenched his teeth; he had to survive this. The amulet throbbed against his chest. He supposed the voices meant to take him and the dragon to the same place. He didn't care anymore.

Except—his skills had returned! When the Golden had escaped through the roof of the cavern, Kurnan had been gripping Lustredust with his knees as if he had always been a dragonrider. His body had adjusted with ease to the demands of dragon flight.

Kurnan sent his thoughts now to Lustredust: *You said we're going to the Cave of Refuge? Where is that?*

No response. A cold darkness hollowed Kurnan's chest. Shivering, he repeated the question. Still no answer. The darkness spread through Kurnan's body. His knees weakened. What was this terrible gloom that gripped him?

Lustredust's wings beat steadily behind him, and the dragon's powerful shoulder muscles rippled under his legs. The end of the short day was closing in. With the thumbside of his palm against his brow, Kurnan squinted into the setting sun. *That's Fossarelick below. Hey, dragon, don't go there.*

Quiet, old fool.

Lustredust passed over the village. Kurnan saw no one around the cottages, nor in the fields. Where were his family and neighbors? The dragon flew on.

Why did you call me a fool?

Aindle, you were always in a hurry.

I'm Kurnan, not Aindle.

And now you think I am the fool.

Kurnan muttered, "Hardly," and stared at the snow-covered mountain peaks ahead of them. "Watch out! See the mouth of that huge cave? There could be dragons."

Just one, my master's enemy. We must destroy him.

Rocánonom

THE CLATTER OF SHATTERING crystal met his first steps into the Cave of Refuge. Rocánonom edged along the cave's stone wall and scanned its broad main chamber. He saw the usual hot stone hearth, a wide nest cushioned with colorful rags, and a neat pile of rodent bones swept into a curved niche.

Distant screams—like those of an enraged dragon—drew his attention to a lighted passageway leading into the cave's depths. Rocánonom's heart quickened with worry and he ran into the passageway.

An iron gate barred him from entering a spacious hall beyond. He pulled at its grillwork, forged into a scene of battling dragons and basilisks, but could not open it. Conjuring a simple access spell, Rocánonom yanked the metalwork again.

That spell succeeded last time I used it. There must be another way in. He searched his memory for a stronger spell. He leaned against a wall supporting one side of the gate. Through the grillwork, he saw a small part of the great observation window the Orferan clan used to survey the Veiled Valley. Only jagged edges of a broken crystal pane remained.

Screams echoed outside the window. Rocánonom felt the blood drain from his face at the sound of creatures battling each other to the death beyond the cave. Vicious roars and snarls smothered weakening dragon groans and yowls. Desperate to release the gate, he banged his fist against the wall behind him. The gate swung open. Stunned, he shook himself out of his daze and ran into the great hall.

Rocánonom stared at the expanse that had once served as the dragons' rear observation post. Gems and shards of crystal blanketed the floor beneath the window sills. He stepped over a broken Silver Dragon statue, as big as himself, its head, body, and wings lying in disarray.

Aurykk's legendary uncle, Argenfort. Pity he's resting in Cold-Turn sleep now. He would have—

An agonized shriek interrupted his musings. Heedless of sharp fragments in his path, Rocánonom ran to the window.

Hovering over Aurykk's still body, which lay on a ledge below, was an enormous Golden. A rider sat astride the dragon's neck hump. *The dragon's eyes—they're white! Which dragon is he?* Rocánonom gasped when he recognized the rider. *Kurnan? Here? But they were following him to the desert.*

The Golden crowed in triumph, spiraled upward into the clouds, and flew sunsetside.

He watched the great beast soar high above the River Valley. *Only a creature ruled by the Malevir would attack Aurykk.* Ahead of the pair was the Coldside Sea. The giant tensed. *If they land on the island, the Malevir will—*but he refused to imagine the consequences. He was supposed to rescue Kurnan but, right now, Aurykk needed his attention. Hoping the venerable Golden still lived, he pulled rope from his kit and rappelled down the cliff face until he reached the wounded dragon.

DRAAKO

His uncle's painful cries flooded his thoughts. Draako beat his wings with a ferocity he had not known since his last battle with the aiglonax. He flexed his front claws. A wingspan away, Isabella's powerful thrusts kept pace with his own. Alana gripped the Copper's frill and hid her face from the cold wind.

Draako squirmed as Nnylf's knees pressed deeply into his neck muscles. He sent his rider reassuring thoughts: *I hear Uncle's calls. Whatever attacked him did not kill him. Hold tight. I'm going to dive. Isabella, following me?*

Of course I am.

The dragons circled above the mouth of the cave. Seeing no sign of Aurykk, they veered away and flew over the mountain's peak. From that height, they searched the span of the mountain range; a broad river valley led to the Coldside Sea.

Do you see them, Draako? There, flying low toward the sea?

No, what do you see, Nnylf?

A dragon and rider—a Golden! Could it really be Lustredust?

Yes, but why is he flying in circles? Isabella said.

Draako winced as Nnylf softly kicked his sides.

Nnylf apologized. *Sorry, my friend, but I see something very strange: four dark funnel clouds whirling around the Golden.*

Air Elementals, ghosts of dragons from before our time.

Alana called out, "They're blocking Lustredust! They've swelled into enormous dragons. He can't get around them."

Yes, the Elementals could stop Lustredust, Isabella said.

"Maybe, but we must help Aurykk now!" Draako blasted out. "He's in pain. Where could he be? Isabella, let's fly lower, by the back chamber."

Draako and Isabella drifted down from the heights. As they flew past the Cave of Refuge's back port, Draako hissed at the sight of widespread devastation. He belched a streak of sour flames when he spotted Aurykk's maimed body splayed across a ledge below the observatory window.

"Isabella, down there, your father!"

"Ways of the World, what happened to him, Draako?" she shrieked.

"He was in a fight. Look, Rocánonom is by his side."

The dragons hung above the fallen Golden, whose legs hung limp across the ledge. Aurykk's tail thrashed then fell with a thud to his heaving side, striped with a trio of deep gashes.

Draako sent his thoughts to Rocánonom, but the giant did not answer. He called again. *Wizarding giant, look up. We are here to help you.*

"I know, I know," Rocánonom answered with a faint growl. "Don't you see I am tending your uncle's wounds? My spells and herbs have stopped the bleeding."

Draako sensed his eyes growing red with anger. He bit his lower lip to calm himself and swallowed the flames struggling to spew from his jaws. *Who did this? Is Aurykk dying?*

"He is alive—barely. Lustredust, his father, tried to kill him. Unnatural beast."

Draako groaned. "Why would he do that?"

"The Malevir ensorcelled him. I can't imagine any other reason. Now look, no more questions. I am doing all I can to help Aurykk. Soon I hope to do more."

"More?"

"Yes, with stronger spells, but first, carry me back to the cave. It needs tidying before we bring Aurykk inside."

Draako watched Isabella circle the giant until she was close enough to grasp his cloak and hoist him into the cave through the shattered port. The roar of a whirlwind followed blinding flashes of light within the cave. Rocánonom's shadow flitted back and forth across the window's blasted frame then stood still. The giant bellowed a string of enchantments until a soft yellow light glowed from inside. The port's dark wooden frame gleamed whole again, and Rocánonom leaned over its edge to call, "I won't bother restoring the crystal pane for now. Bring Aurykk up here to me."

Draako looked at Isabella. Her eyes were wild and red.

Nnylf nudged Draako with his heel. "You know you two are strong enough. Use your forelegs and carry him as you once carried poor Kurnan to the shelter of the great oak long ago, but first, lighten your load. Take Alana and me back to the cave entrance."

Draako bit his lower lip again and bent his head to the task. The dragons flew to the cave's front opening. After giving their riders directions to the back chamber, they left them on the ledge and returned to Aurykk.

Before long, they managed to fly his massive body up to the port, where Rocánonom used an old wooden rod to guide the Golden onto a fresh nest lying in the middle of the chamber.

After Aurykk was settled into the nest and looked as if he were sleeping, the giant leaned out the port. "Now, you and your riders, trail Lustredust. Keep him away from the Coldside Sea Island. We will follow you when I see that Aurykk has recovered enough to fly."

Isabella snorted. "That will take too long." Alana was climbing up the Copper's side.

"Not so long. I have a way to speed the healing."

Seated on his dragon's hump, Nnylf whispered, "Tell him about the dragon spirits."

Draako looked at the giant, bent over one of Aurykk's wounds. "Oh yes. Rocánonom, you mentioned the Coldside Sea. Well, we saw some sort of dragon spirits, maybe Elementals, circling around the ghost dragon. Will they stop him?"

"If they are Elementals, they won't hold him there for long, not if the Malevir controls him. I met them on my way here. I told them about the Malevir. I think they are ready to help us."

Draako's wings quivered. What would the Malevir do with Kurnan?

"Try your best to delay Lustredust." Rocánonom looked up. "Kurnan must not reach the Malevir's stronghold."

Draako wanted to stay with Aurykk, but he raged against Lustredust's senseless violence and was eager to go after him. A great cloud of worry fogged his thoughts, and he remembered Isabella. She would know what to do. He turned to ask her a question, but she was not there. He heard Alana cry out. Nnylf patted his neck and pointed toward the Coldside Sea.

"Isabella and Alana are on their way. Leave your uncle to the giant's preternatural powers. Let's go now," he shouted.

Hold tight. My rage clouds my sight. Do your best to guide me. Draako nodded to the giant, flipped his tail, and hurried to catch up to his cousin.

Part 6

Journey's End

NNYLF
AND
ALANA

Enderfon

THE ROCK GIANT TOSSED Rowel, his bejeweled mace, from one hand to the other as he walked toward the Sunsetside Mountains. Sweetnettle flitted between the giant's shoulders and whispered the latest news in his ear. "The chary bird brought a message from Rocánonom. Lustredust attacked his son Aurykk outside the Cave of Refuge."

"That ancient lump of lizardry has a death wish, I think."

"Death wish? Aurykk or Lustredust?"

"Lustredust. He never had his Twilight Time, you know."

"Why?"

"Treachery killed him. I met him long before people settled in the Veiled Valley. Did Rocánonom say Lustredust's ghost killed Aurykk?"

"He said Aurykk lives and will heal. Why did you say Lustredust has a death wish?"

Enderfon slowed his pace and held out a craggy palm. Sweetnettle landed on it and sat on a jutting thumb joint. "My little friend, wouldn't you wish to escape the Malevir? Lustredust sees only one way to do that—by giving up the ghost, so to speak. Though I'm sure the beast forced him to attack Aurykk, just for spite."

Sweetnettle shook his head and wiped a tear. "I have news from Draako and Isabella too. They are following Kurnan toward the Coldside Sea. Some Air Elementals tried to stop Lustredust, but he flew right through them!"

"Where's he going?"

"To the island, they think."

Enderfon studied the Lobli for a few moments then whispered, "I'll have to move faster if we're to help our friends and Kurnan. Tuck yourself in here." He placed the little sprite inside a rocky hollow between his neck and shoulder. "No more flying as we go. I'll tell you my story to make the journey more interesting."

"Rowel's story, too?"

"Yes. You know Rowel has great powers. You saw how life-giving it is."

Sweetnettle nodded. Enderfon's rough lips curled in a soft smile. *He's probably remembering the food I prepared for him when we first met.*

"When I lived on the edge of the Warmside Beyond, I awoke one cloudless night to raucous calls. Circling above me in the moonlight was a flokk of many, many dragons. Their golden leader swooped down and sat facing me like a king on his throne. Soon a Bronze Dragon dam glided in and sat next to the dragon leader. They stared at me without saying anything, not a sigh, a growl, nor a coil of smoke. I thought a World-Turn had passed when, from under her wing, the dam pulled out Rowel and offered it to me.

"'Here, take it for safe-keeping, giant. We trust you will keep it with you always. We need your help. With this mace, you can give us that help,' she said.

"Her words flabbergasted me, but I took the mace and felt its heft. I remember saying silly things like, 'Solid, this is. Pretty, too.' I admired the gems sticking out of it. Then I asked, 'Who are you?'"

"Should have asked that in the first place." Sweetnettle yawned.

"Well, the dam said she was Eminfoil, and her mate was named Lustredust."

"*That* Lustredust?"

"Yes, and I asked them why they wanted me to have the mace. What was I to do with it? Eminfoil said, 'It has great power, so guard it with your life. Keep it out of the wrong hands. Use it to bring life to the land and comfort to its creatures, for soon they are coming to the Veiled Valley, their new home. Our home, too.'

"Finally, the Golden moved. He lifted his splendid wings and showed me a small glowing box nestled in his claws. 'This holds the Mystic Scintilla, wrapped in the hide of our most ancient forefather. Its light brings strength and healing. Rowel's gems and power—power for life, but also for destruction—come from the Mystic Scintilla. Use the mace wisely.'

"The two dragons stood, preparing to leap up and join their flokk, but I stopped them to ask, 'Where are you going with that box?' The dam touched her snout to her mate's before answering. 'See our flokk above us? Each dragon carries some of our treasure hoard. We are taking the treasure and the Mystic Scintilla to our new lair, on the sunrise side of the Veiled Valley. Someday young dragons, our descendants, will call it the Cave of the Ancestors.'

"Little did they know the Malevir's treachery would kill them. Anyway, after those words, the two dragons flew off."

Sweetnettle rubbed his eyes before mumbling, "Poor Lustredust." Enderfon soon heard the jagged sound of Sweetnettle's snores. He marched on, toward the Coldside Sea.

KURNAN

KURNAN TIGHTENED HIS GRIP on the Golden's frill. His back and arms ached. Lustredust's struggle against battering winds had rubbed his legs raw. He glanced past the dragon's tail, slashing the air in its wake. The shore was far behind them. Looking ahead, Kurnan gasped. They were crossing the Coldside Sea and approaching an island. Its lofty towers gleamed, despite the dim light of day. A broad portal gaped at the base of the towers, dark and lifeless.

He shivered, remembering another portal this dragon had destroyed a short while ago. Smashing into ancient Aurykk's inner chamber, Lustredust had attacked with open jaws. Kurnan clung to the ghost dragon, too frightened to scream or look away. His heart pounded as Lustredust tossed the startled dragon through the broad window and dived at him, hanging onto a ledge below. Why did Aurykk snarl and bare his fangs but not defend himself? The Malevir must have given Lustredust extraordinary powers.

Kurnan clung to Lustredust's frill while the ghost dragon's talons tore at Aurykk's belly scales and limbs. The raging beast's fury made his stomach heave, but Lustredust ignored him and his bile. The furious Golden pummeled and pounded Aurykk until his victim stopped moving and his eyes fluttered closed. Lustredust then turned and flew toward the Coldside Sea.

Terrified to be riding a killer dragon intent on reaching the grim and foreboding island ahead of them, Kurnan could not clear his jumbled thoughts. Why were they here? Why attack a peaceful dragon and wreck his lair? The voices had promised him a haven overlooking the desert, not a descent into madness and murder.

The amulet was pressing against his clothes like a hot coal. He tried to pull it away, but it scorched his palm. Kurnan cooled his hand in the streaming air; the amulet tucked itself back into his jerkin.

At that moment, deep in his head, a small chorus of voices began to chant. He could barely hear them. Then they returned with a roar so loud Kurnan wanted to clamp his hands to his ears.

You are home, Kurnan. You are home. YOU ARE HOME.

Lustredust lifted his wings. He rolled and yawed. Kurnan leaned into the frill and clasped as much of Lustredust's neck as he could. The voices roared again.

ENTER.

Lustredust flew low until he was level with the enormous, dark rocks that circled the island. Squatting on a rock curiously shaped like a sleeping dragon, Lustredust rested for a few moments, sniffed the rock, then sprang upward with an agonized wail until he reached the highest point of the island, the summit of a tower made of ice and stone.

ROCÁNONOM

THE ATTACK WEAKENED ME, but I'm strong enough to blast my flames at you. What are you looking for?" Aurykk growled. His head sank back into the foliage and rags lining his nest. He sighed and rolled his eyes in Rocánonom's direction.

"Begging your pardon, wise one, but I did leave something hidden here many World-Turns ago."

"Oh, *that*. We'd all be better off keeping it hidden. In fact, I should have burned it before you could hide it."

The magician giant strolled to the nest, put his hands on his hips, and cocked his head. "Your wounds ache and burn, don't they, even after I tended to them."

"Well, yes, it'll take them a while to heal, I suppose. My heart will take longer to mend."

"You don't have 'a while' because you're needed on Coldside Sea Island—now."

Aurykk lifted his massive head and raised himself on his forelegs. "*I* am needed?"

"The Malevir controls Lustredust's spirit and made him attack you. Now the beast summons him to his tower on the island."

The Golden snorted cinders and shook his head. "Not the true Lustredust. He died. That was my father's ghost."

"Rather, a dragon spirit trapped between life and death. The Malevir commands Kurnan too."

"I know, with that wretched amulet."

"Worse, he's riding Lustredust."

Aurykk's forelegs buckled, and his head lay over the edge of the nest. "Then Dragonwolder is lost."

Rocánonom pointed to the cave wall. "Not if I use what I hid in that niche."

Aurykk's eyes were half closed. "What niche?"

"That ell-shaped cut in the rock where I hid the book of spells."

"Ah, so that's where it's been. How will you use it?"

"Carefully. I'll need to study it. What I learn for now will heal you quickly, and then…"

"And then?"

"You'll see."

ALANA

W E HAVE TO LAND. I feel sick!" Alana called to Nnylf. Sharp pains knifed her stomach, and she was sure she would lose everything she'd eaten since leaving Kurnan's cave. She wiped sweat from her brow. Her right temple throbbed. *What's the matter with me? I'm never sick. Well, almost never.*

Hold on, dear friend. We'll rest a bit on the shore before we cross the sea, Isabella said. Draako nodded and the dragons began their descent.

Nnylf looked worried. Good. Alana wanted him to care. Her fears were growing as they flew closer to the Coldside Sea and its grim island. She wanted so much to rescue her brother, but what more could they do after the Elementals menaced Lustredust and failed to stop him? She needed time to think. If only she could talk calmly with Nnylf and figure out what to do, but she could not tame the fears clouding her thoughts.

Isabella glided along the shore, and Draako arrived moments later. Nnylf jumped quickly to the pebbled beach. Holding her breath, Alana watched him run toward her. When Nnylf reached her, he cupped her cheek in his palm. She could not hold back her tears.

"Oh, Nnylf, I am so frightened—for Kurnan and for ourselves. The tower looks so...so..."

"Dangerous?"

She nodded and blew her nose into the rag Nnylf offered her. "The Malevir, he's there, probably stirring up endless dark enchantments. What will happen if we follow Lustredust all the way into the Malevir's keep? Will Isabella and Draako protect us?"

Nnylf wrapped an arm around her shoulders. Without thinking, she leaned into him and studied his face. How strong he looked. His big brown eyes, shaded with dark lashes, were searching her own.

"Thank you, my stomach's settled a bit," she whispered, enjoying the body warmth radiating through his armor. "You make me feel a whole lot safer."

Nnylf slipped the cap from her head and stroked her hair. She blinked as he said, "You're the one who makes me feel strong. You're so smart and caring. I've learned so much from you." He bent toward her and kissed her lightly on her cheek.

That was nice. I wonder what his lips taste like. Alana turned her head and brushed Nnylf's rough lips with her own. *Umm, more.* She kissed him again and felt his hands grip her shoulders.

"I...I didn't know you cared for me that much."

Alana's heart leaped. "I do, I mean, I have, for a long time, I guess. It's just, well, we've had other things to think about."

Nnylf smiled and returned her cap. "Speaking of which, we have a brother to rescue." A swift hug and he was leaping onto Draako's rider's hump. "If you're feeling better, we should go."

Too bad. You're so nice to be near.

Isabella broke into her thoughts. *I heard that, dear friend. Come, we really should go. Kurnan's life depends on us.*

Alana gulped and shook her head to clear her thoughts. *What's wrong with me? Of course, we will go. That's the point of this journey. Isabella, I'm ready.*

Alana hoisted herself up to her Copper's rider's hump, and the dragons shot into the air, leaving the shore behind them.

KURNAN

THE AMULET THROBBED IN angry waves against Kurnan's chest. As if he, too, felt its power, Lustredust landed with a jolt on the pinnacle of an ice tower. Kurnan tightened his grip on the dragon's frill. Despite the voices' reassurances, an acrid taste of gut-deep fear filled Kurnan's mouth. Everything was wrong here. Something was also very wrong with Lustredust.

The dragon's dark thoughts jumbled his own. Kurnan's mind was like a mass of thunderheads. He could not separate himself from the storm churning inside the creature.

Lustredust descended into the tower. *We've reached the end of everything. My Eminfoil, lost to me forever.* His flight spiraled downward. He circled a dark, tree-like column, the tower's central support; its upper branches looked like spires sheathed in glistening stones and icicles.

Kurnan reached out to him: *Tell me, where are you going?*

My master calls.

The Golden followed a curved wall surrounding the column. Its gleaming surface blinded Kurnan. He shielded his eyes from the glare but could not resist peeking through his fingers. His throat closed, and he barely breathed. The ice wall encased more dragons—too many to count—of all colors, yet translucent. Kurnan could see daylight passing through them.

Lustredust settled without a sound. A tremor rippled from the Golden's head to his tail; it shook Kurnan and sent him tumbling to the thick blue-ice floor. On his hands and knees, Kurnan stared at enormous black rocks lying under the frozen mass. They looked like the curved rock he had seen earlier, the one shaped like a sleeping dragon.

The floor shuddered. Lustredust was moving away from him, past the column, toward the ice wall. His head drooped at the end of his long neck, and his tattered wings hung close to the floor. His scales were graying.

"Wait!" Kurnan called after him. "Don't leave me."

The dragon swung his head to face Kurnan. His white eyes blinked in puzzlement. *I must go now.*

"You can't leave me." Kurnan's breaths came short and fast. He watched the dragon lumber across the floor and settle into a recess in the wall. The space fit him perfectly, as if it had been waiting for him. Ice crystals began to flake off the wall above the Golden and cling to his dull scales. Horrified, yet fascinated, Kurnan watched the crystals harden around Lustredust until they covered him completely.

I feel nothing now. No pain. No sorrow. Only regret.

"What do you regret?"

Attacking my son.

"You can't leave me. We can go back. We can help him!" Kurnan shouted as he fought his tears and ran to Lustredust. Like a door slamming in his face, the ice wall encasing Lustredust smashed into Kurnan. The young rider had never felt so alone.

You're not alone. We are with you.

He startled. The voices re-entered his head and, with them, a pain that squeezed his temples. He shouted, "With me? Ha! You're against me. Otherwise, you—"

We are *with you. You have a new purpose.*

Kurnan's eyes were full of tears again, and a huge lump kept him from swallowing. "What new purpose? You promised to protect—"

Lustredust did protect you.

"He almost killed me. Why did he bring me here?"

Quiet! Too many questions.

"I *demand* to know." Although chilled, Kurnan felt his face redden with rage and torment.

You are the star they seek.

"I'm no star. You make no sense. You promised me—"

Nothing but pain and shame.

"What? You promised my pain and my shame would end. You said the amulet would protect me. What about my miserable trek across the Veiled Valley and those uprooter attacks? What about my aching body?" Kurnan clenched his fists. *I still have some strength.* He waited.

The voices did not answer. Weary with fever, sweat pooling under his chin, Kurnan pulled at his tunic. His hand brushed the amulet. "You said I would be nothing until I left Fossarelick—but this, this *thing* brought me nothing—nothing but grief." He yanked the amulet off and threw it. With a life of its own, the amulet spun in small circles and clattered against the column. "Take it back. Let me go home. I want to go home to Fossarelick."

A wave of weariness washed over him. Drawing his fingers through his dark hair, Kurnan massaged his scalp. His head stopped throbbing. The voices remained silent.

Bone-tired, Kurnan rubbed his eyes with his palms. *I did cross the valley. I did survive attacks. Why should I feel shame? Didn't I ride a ghost dragon as well as I used to fly with Isabella? And I survived.* Kurnan's throat tightened and a wave of grief flooded him. *Isabella, my dear Copper. Why did I shut you out of my life? I miss you.*

Kurnan looked at Lustredust's frozen tomb. *He thought I was his rider. Aindle betrayed him, but he came back here. Why?*

Lustredust came here to die, a gravelly voice resounded.

The voice surprised him. It was outside his head. Kurnan whirled around, hoping to find its source.

He came here to die. Now, you will too.

The amulet floated past him. He watched it wind its way up the column, into its highest branches, then disappear. A sharp pain stabbed Kurnan's ears. He squeezed his eyes shut and covered his ears. When he opened his eyes, he cringed at the sight of a large dark object quickly falling from the tower's peak. He tried to run; his boots were stuck, frozen to the floor. He yanked at his legs. They would not budge. Before he could look up again, a cage dropped over him and burned its edges into the floor.

Steam rose all around him. Kurnan pulled his feet out of his boots and shuddered as melting ice water soaked his leggings. He was trapped. The bars of the cage glowed fiery red. He banged the flat of his hand against a bar and screamed. His palm was badly burned. Kurnan pressed it against the floor to deaden the pain.

"Why have you done this? You promised to protect me." Kurnan's rasping words echoed from the tower walls. "You have your amulet. Let me go back to Fossarelick."

No. They will come now, and they will die.

ISABELLA

I HEAR HIM!" ISABELLA SCREAMED. "Is that really him?"

Alana's knees dug into her hump. "What *him*? Who'd you hear?"

"Your brother, I hope." Isabella spewed cinders. "I heard his thoughts, but why now, after such a long silence? What's happened to him?" She nodded to Draako, who followed her as she circled the island. *I know Kurnan is there, perhaps in the tower.*

The Malevir's hold on Kurnan must have weakened, but you know we can't go in there, Draako said.

But… Desperation tortured Isabella.

No.

Alana interrupted the dragons' thoughts. *Why not?*

No dragon may enter.

But why? You're so powerful, Draako. Both of you surely—

Not powerful enough to leave the tower.

Nnylf faced Alana and shouted, "Then you and I will go!"

"Nnylf, no, not you. I don't want harm to come to you. I'll go alone. I should be helping my brother."

"No, Alana."

The two riders argued until the dragons landed on the rocky shore of the island. Alana slid to the ground. She looked up at Isabella, stumbling as she stepped back. "You are snorting cinders, my friend, and your eyes are red."

Isabella roared, "Of course they're red! I feel so angry, so sad! My father battered by that ghost dragon—my grandsire! And Kurnan's in danger. I sense his racing heartbeat. I am helpless to save him."

Draako lowered his head close to the two riders. "Isabella and I cannot enter this place. Oh, anyone can enter, but dragons never leave. They go there to die. Our instincts tell us to stay away if we want to live." He belched a cloud of gray smoke, and the riders bent over, coughing.

As soon as Alana and Nnylf breathed easily again, Isabella said, "The Malevir is here. He wants to trap us inside to die with our ancestors. I feel it, as strong and bitter as when Kurnan and I battled the aiglonax." She hissed, "I hear your brother, I hear his thoughts again." She dropped to the ground, covered her head with her claws, and howled, "Fuzzy thoughts; he's boxed in somehow. O, Ways of the World, help us. He needs me."

She needed a comforting pat from Alana. Lowering her forelegs, Isabella waited for her rider's words but felt no touch, heard no soothing sounds. Alana and Nnylf were facing the tower. They hugged and searched each other's eyes. Isabella heard Nnylf whisper in the young woman's ear, "Stay close. Be careful. We'll find him." They left the shore, climbed the rocks, and walked a sandy path toward the tower. *Humph, not even a 'bye, see you later,'* Isabella grumbled.

She turned around at the sound of claws scraping on rocks. Draako was standing by her side. She welcomed his closeness. She could feel anxious heat rising from his scales. "Did you hear the spirits of our ancestors, too, or am I now a spirit myself?"

Draako pressed his fangs into his lower lip and sank down beside her. "You are very much alive. May the Ways of the World protect us all."

AURYKK

AURYKK'S PAINS LESSENED WITH every passing moment. He rolled to his side and watched the magician giant flick through a few heavy pages of his grimoire. *What does he hope to find? I feel nearly whole again. His last spell worked a cure on those gashes. What more could he want?*

As if Rocánonom were reading Aurykk's mind, he answered aloud, "I saw it here many World-Turns ago, a spell designed not only to call but also master the Elementals. That is what I need. What *we* need."

"Mastery, you mean total control? I have many powers, but nothing like that. Sorry." He settled back on his belly.

"You have untapped powers, my friend. We need total control over just one kind of Elemental, who will obey my commands. The spell should be here. I remember seeing it once."

Rocánonom slid his index finger across a sheet of parchment, shook his head, and sighed. After turning a few more pages, his finger paused in midair. Releasing a long, slow breath, he tapped a block of handwritten text on the page before him. "Here it is, the very spell I seek." Drawings wreathed the text—diaphanous dragons, tinted brown, watery-blue, madder-red, and gray.

"Aurykk, I need your help to say and understand a few unfamiliar marks. The author of the grimoire wrote in the Common Tongue, but here he used ancient dragon runes, including some I've never seen." The giant cradled the book in his arms and carried it to Aurykk's nest. "For example, look at this. It's next to the mark meaning 'clean.'"

Aurykk raised his head then pushed himself up until he was sitting on his haunches, his tail wrapped closely around him. "Give it here. Let me see."

After clearing his nose of bothersome soot, Aurykk examined the text. "Apologies. I need a few moments to adjust my inner sight." He paused and breathed deeply. "Ah, there it is. Yes, I see. It does say 'clean,' referring to a clean heart. Show me which marks are unfamiliar."

The giant pointed out the runes puzzling him. He drew a sheet of smooth, pounded bark from his pouch and waited, his writing stick ready to take notes. Aurykk translated all but one set of runes, an arrangement he had never seen before.

"Odd, this cluster. Let me sit quietly with it for a bit."

Rocánonom leaned back against the rim of the nest and closed his eyes. "Aurykk, old friend, this is so much trouble, but so worth it. The spell will bind the Fire Elemental to me until I summon the antidote, another spell, written below the runes in Common Tongue. If you can't break the runic code to master the Elemental, how can we confront the Malevir?" He mopped beads of sweat from his brow with the edge of a sleeve. Impatient, he jumped to his feet and peered over Aurykk's snout to look at the text. A drop of sweat fell directly on the mystery runes.

"Good work!" Aurykk called out. "Your sweat unraveled the marks. Now they make sense."

Rocánonom laughed. "Well, what do they mean?"

"They stand for Fyreburn, the Elemental Dragon of Fire. Fyreburn, uh-hum." Aurykk drifted into his own musings while Rocánonom hurried to write down the spell and its instructions.

"The word isn't 'clean,' by the way."

"But I thought—"

"The word also means 'pure,' and..."

"And?"

"Taken all together, the text instructs the spellbinder to sing the enchantment while astride a Golden Dragon. Who could that be?" he said with a wink.

"You are the only *living* Golden, Aurykk. So, you see, to be effective the spell needs both of us. Will you do it?"

"Yes, but not as I am right now."

Rocánonom slipped his notes and writing stick into the pouch and flicked through the grimoire's pages again. "Thank you. I'll use one more spell—it's here somewhere—and you'll feel like a young dragon of merely a hundred World-Turns—for a while, at least long enough for us to complete our task."

"I'd like that."

Rocánonom found the spell and pronounced it in a deep voice. Aurykk's lips curled in a grin, and his yellow fangs turned gleaming white. He rose from his nest, stretched his hind legs, and was about to unfurl his wings.

"Wait, wait," the giant called out. "Let me give you some room."

Aurykk, feeling young and strong again, paraded around the broad chamber. "Giant, when do we leave for the Coldside Sea Island?"

"As soon as the grimoire is safely hidden."

"Don't let me see where you hide it. I'm closing my eyes and covering my ears. My thoughts are like porridge. Na-nah-nah-nah." Aurykk's heart was beating with newfound force, and he was eager to fly again. "Hurry. We have much to do," he said as the giant scrambled up his side and settled into the Golden's rider's hump.

"I'm ready, Aurykk. Why are you standing still? Let's move."

"Rocánonom, I hear my daughter, Isabella. Grief is tearing her apart."

"Then we've no time to waste," the giant cried and bent into Aurykk's frill as the dragon leaped out the portal and unfurled his bright wings with newfound power.

NNYLF

BLOCKS OF ICE, SOME as big as his family's cottage, surrounded the frozen tower. Nnylf's teeth chattered, and he longed for a blast of Draako's warm breath. Alana's cold hand gripped his own as he pulled her up and over the frozen terrain toward the tower's entrance. It would be nice to stop here, warm her hands, and hold her close, but that would have to wait, provided she wanted him to hold her close.

No door sealed the dark arched entrance to the tower where Nnylf stopped to face Alana.

"Please stay out here and wait for me. No reason both of us should risk meeting up with the beast."

"Have you lost your mind, Nnylf? There's reason aplenty. Kurnan is my brother. He needs to see me. He won't recognize you anyway. You've changed so much since he last saw you." She smiled. "And for the better." Alana's smile slipped into a hardened grimace. "I'm going in there to free Kurnan."

Nnylf's heart sank. If he could, he would send her back to Isabella, but Alana was determined. "Fine, but you don't *have* to go. Kurnan's illness was not your fault."

Alana's chin dropped, and a tear dissolved the snowflakes coating her cheek. "I know. It's just that, well, he was so young when the aiglonax poisoned him. I wish it had been me."

His arms enfolded her and drew her close until her head rested against his chest. *Well, I didn't expect that so soon.* If they hadn't been wearing armor, he'd have pressed even closer. As he stroked her soft curls, she lifted her face and drew his down. "Kiss me, Nnylf, just in case. It might be our last…"

Nnylf gulped. *All right!* He cupped Alana's burning face in his numb hands. His fingers began to thaw. Her lips were warm too, and her eagerness to return the kiss surprised him. He pulled back. "You and I are more than friends, I guess."

Alana's smile reassured him. She answered in a whisper. "Yeah, I guess. It's a little weird."

"We'll go in there together, Alana, and when we bring Kurnan home…" Nnylf regretted their next move. How much easier it would be to find their dragons and return home without Kurnan, although he'd feel terrible about it. He looked at the entrance then back at Alana. Her grim face, with a knot between her eyebrows, said it all, as if she had read his mind.

She stepped back, tightened her pack, and pulled her cap snugly over her ears. "Yes, we are going to bring him home. Let's go."

Nnylf nodded and pointed to his chest. He intended to enter the tower first, but Alana brushed past him. He reached for her sleeve, but she hurried ahead. She glided across the icy floor, like a skater on a frozen pond, toward a boxlike cage opposite the entrance. He hesitated only a moment before slipping and sliding after her.

Scraping her heel into the glossy surface, Alana stopped halfway across the room and stared at the tower wall surrounding them. "Nnylf, do you see them?"

He gawked at dragons of all hues and sizes, trapped in the wall's stones and ice. One caught his eye. "Alana, look over there. A Golden.

Not quite covered in ice. Snow crystals are coating his head and frill."

"If that's Lustredust, Kurnan would be... He is! I see him in that cage. Hurry!"

Almost reaching the far side of the tower, Nnylf and Alana skidded into each other and, limbs flying out, they fell with a thud to the floor. Nnylf found himself splayed across Alana's backside, and she muttered, "Nnylf, get *off*!" He sighed inwardly; she used to say that when they played tag as kids.

"Hey! Alana, watch out. The cage—" Kurnan's hoarse voice pulled them apart, but too late to escape another red-hot cage falling over them. The trap's bottom edge sizzled as it sank into the blue ice below. Kurnan shouted a warning about the metal bars, and Nnylf cringed at his friend's cry.

Alana stared through the bars at her brother. "Kurnan, we came to free you. Don't worry. We'll all be free soon. Our dragons will help us, and we'll go back to the Veiled Valley."

Nnylf whispered, "Alana, how can you give him such false hopes? You know Isabella and Draako said they would never enter this tower."

"Then just what *are* we going to do?" Her answer echoed around the tower.

"YOU CAN DO NOTHING," boomed a voice from the heights.

Nnylf searched the upper stretches of the wall and the open spires at the top of the tower but saw no one. "Who are you? What do you want?" he called out.

Alana's shoulder pressed into his own. She reached for his hand and gripped it tightly. After whispering to him, "Your hand is so cold," she called out to the voice, "What have you done to my brother?"

"I'm all right, Alana. How did you find me?" Kurnan shouted before the voice cut him off.

"FOR NOW."

Nnylf's anger boiled up and, on impulse, he reached for the cage bars.

"I told you, don't touch the bars!" screamed Kurnan. "They burn!" Nnylf pulled back his hand.

"Is there no way out? We're trapped in here, just like Kurnan."

"TRAPPED. YES. UNTIL THEY COME."

"Until who comes?" Nnylf shouted as he continued to look high and low for the voice's source.

"THE DRAGONS."

"They won't come," Nnylf muttered. *They said they can't. Now I can see why. They didn't want to join the others, frozen in the wall.*

I hear you, Nnylf.

Alana! You?

Yes, so the Malevir can't hear us. My legs are so tired. There's no place to sit but the ice.

Mine, too. Come here. Lean on me.

Alana's warm back comforted him. He could feel her relax a bit until another thought struck her.

Who knows how long Kurnan has been in that cage. Is he starving?

Nnylf hid a grin at the sound of Alana's stomach gurgles. Wishing their other companions were with them, he grimaced at the swarm of buzzing, anxious thoughts in his head, all of his own making: Would Enderfon and Sweetnettle soon arrive at the Coldside Sea's shore? How could they cross the water and reach the island? And had Rocánonom's magic healed Aurykk? Would they find a way to rescue him and his friends? What was that awful voice? Where was it hiding?

SWEETNETTLE

As HE MADE HIS way from the Coldside Desert to the sea, every step the rock giant took jostled his Lobli passenger. Hanging onto stony outcrops in a cranny between Enderfon's neck and chest, Sweetnettle sang little tunes to warm himself, but fierce winter winds seeped through his clothing despite magick meant to seal them from wind and rain. He shouted up toward the giant's ear. "Enderfon, I'm freezing down here. Can you use Rowel somehow to warm me up?"

Enderfon whispered, "You know I can't. Don't you remember Eminfoil's warning? She said, 'Rowel has great power, so guard it with your life. Keep it out of the wrong hands. Use it to bring life to the land and comfort to its creatures, for soon they are coming to the Veiled Valley, their new home.'"

"Exactly, if you'd be so kind. You can bring comfort to me, a little creature, chilled to the bone. Remember, you fed me back at the needlerock."

"Ha! She didn't mean it that way, my tiny friend, but I do want to help you."

"Please hurry then. My fingers are numb, and I can't feel my nose."

"We're close to Anonom Trace. If the fog hereabouts hasn't hidden it and fooled me, the Loblin manor house should be close by."

With his next few long strides, Enderfon crossed a series of rolling hills and reached a low dale. He offered Sweetnettle his hand and lowered him gently to the ground in front of a broad green door in the middle of a large windowless building.

"Go ahead, knock. You'll have a pleasant surprise."

Sweetnettle knew this place, but it had been so long... He tapped the door with one finger. It swung open. The entrance was dark and Sweetnettle hesitated. "Enderfon, do you think I'll like what I find here?"

The rock giant's chuckles reverberated like thunder. "Certain of it."

"Very well. Where will you be?"

"I will wait for you, right here." Enderfon lowered himself to the ground. His body resembled a jumble of boulders, except for his mouth and sparkling eyes. "Go on." He waved the back of his hand toward the entrance.

Sweetnettle shrugged and stepped inside. At his second step, a chorus of giggles greeted him. Four small figures his own size stepped out of the shadows and surrounded him. A soft gray light spread through the vestibule, and Sweetnettle gaped with surprise at the Loblin standing there.

"Close your mouth, Sweetnettle, and come join us at our table," said a red-haired Lobli, bouncy curls escaping his loose green cap.

"Jink! You're here." Sweetnettle's astonishment took his breath away, especially after seeing the faces of the other three Loblin. "Purfle...Footle." His eyes next met those of the tallest sprite, dressed in leather leggings and a brown vest woven from meadow grasses. "And Pilgarlic. How I have missed you all!" He gazed with affection at his old friends.

"We've been guarding this safe house so long it feels like forever. The Malevir can't touch us if we—and you—are inside. Rocánonom brought us here and magicked the place, and we open it to all who need shelter from the Malevir."

"I remember that. We were inspecting the village of Anonom Trace. Something told Rocánonom the Malevir was near. He pushed you four inside, cast a protective spell over this manse and, with the rest of us, dashed off toward the Sunriseside Mountains to reach the dragons' cave. The Malevir's hork caught up with us and turned us into slave goblins before we could escape."

"Rocánonom, too."

"Yes, he ended up beaten, gagged, and chained in a mountain dungeon until we goblins found him much, much later. We freed each other from the Malevir's spells. Thank the Ways of the World you were spared all that."

The other two Loblin, twins wearing leafy caps, stroked their little braided beards; then they took Sweetnettle by the hand and led him to a table set with plates, goblets, and spoons. They invited him to sit on a padded stool and help himself to bowls of berries, roasted acorns, and platters of breads and cakes.

"We're so sorry you suffered. Rocánonom was here not long ago. He left for the Cave of Refuge. He was in a hurry and left in the middle of the night."

"Do you know where he is now?" Sweetnettle's stomach growled. He quieted it with several bites of cake. "Did he reach the cave?"

Pilgarlic brushed breadcrumbs off his green- and brown-dotted tunic. "We don't know. Why are *you* here, brother? We're happy to see you, but…"

"My friend Enderfon the rock giant brought me here to warm up, I think."

"Enderfon? We thought he was just a story."

"No, he's very real. He has a powerful mace, Rowel. Enderfon and I are going to the Coldside Sea to help fight the Malevir again. You should come with us. Together, we might have enough magick to save Dragonwolder from another Malevir attack."

The Loblin's eyes grew wide. Jink apologized. They had to stay in the manor house. Footle suggested that they might have other ways of helping, and Purfle nodded with vigor. "We do, we do!" he shouted. "The curtain."

His twin, Footle, looked at him, his brow puckered in puzzlement. "What curtain?"

"The one we used to hide ourselves at the end of Rocánonom's last visit. Remember, he couldn't find us?"

"Oh, *that* curtain." Footle ran out of the room and soon returned with a big bundle clutched in his arms. "This looks like an ordinary bit of black drapery, but flip it in front of you, like laundry set out to dry, and no one sees you coming."

Sweetnettle left his stool, placed his goblet on the table, and stood next to Footle.

"Why will this help?"

"The Malevir will feel as if someone is near him, but the cloak will totally befuddle him. Watch." Footle stepped back, across the room from Sweetnettle. He unfolded the black cloth and snapped it in the air in front of him. "You have to snap it three times." After two more snaps, Footle and the cloth disappeared.

"Are you still here?" Sweetnettle whispered.

"I'll roll it up now." Footle's legs appeared, followed by the rest of his body, and the black sheet lay rolled up across his arms. "See? Easy. It also works as a screen. You can see out of it, but no one on the other side can see in."

Sweetnettle's grin nearly split his face. "I forgot about the magical curtain. Thank you. It will be a big help. Now all we need is a way to reach the Coldside Sea Island."

Pilgarlic stretched his long arms and scratched his bare pate. "If the stories about Enderfon are true, you will have no problem getting there, but don't leave yet. Have another bite or two and drink our rue broth. You never know…"

"Oh, yes, the rue broth, a powerful brew. It protected me so many times from the Malevir's poisons. Thank you." He raised his goblet to his lips and guzzled down the brew. After gobbling a few more cakes, he straightened his tunic and flicked a few crumbs from his belly. "I'll be on my way, then?"

"The curtain's in your pack and a few more cakes. Let us walk you to the door."

The four sprites accompanied Sweetnettle up the stairs and, with a little whistle, summoned open the green door. Sweetnettle invited them to meet Enderfon, but duty called; they insisted on remaining in the manse. They hugged each other fiercely, and Sweetnettle walked across the threshold toward Enderfon. The door creaked shut behind him.

ENDERFON

THE ROCK GIANT'S PEBBLY skin registered Sweetnettle's slight weight as the sprite sat perched on his shoulder. Enderfon cautioned him to hang on tightly as he lengthened his stride and pace. His sharp hearing picked up voices coming from the Coldside Sea Island. He recognized Draako's growl and Isabella's cries of despair, but faint, muffled calls from people he did not recognize puzzled him. Nnylf and Alana were with their dragons, weren't they? He ought to hear their words just as clearly as he heard the dragons.

Enderfon struggled against his slow-moving joints. Isabella's despair speeded him on as best he could. *If only I were more flesh than stone, I would be nimbler.* He smiled. *But if I were more flesh than stone, I would not be this strong. Perhaps it is for the better.*

A short time later, Enderfon reached the seashore. Sweetnettle was batting his earlobe with his braided belt. "Enderfon, I can't fly as far as the island, and you'll sink to the bottom of the sea. The waves are churning. We could drown."

The giant offered Sweetnettle his open palm. After the sprite settled into the least uncomfortable part of it, Enderfon raised him to his face and whispered, "We talked about Rowel and its power to build the land. Do you remember?"

Sweetnettle nodded.

"Perch on my shoulder now and watch Rowel work her magick."

Enderfon's confidence did not match his words, but he hefted his mace and raised it in the air. Lining up its gems with the island far across the water, he chanted:

> Sunbeams, moon glow, and spidery lace
> Come to my Rowel, the magical mace.
> Akin to the treasure that dragons still hoard
> Add to her power and
> Work in accord.

At first, only blustery shore winds jostled Rowel, but soon Enderfon needed to tighten his grip. The mace shivered in his hands. Its rubies and sapphires glowed red and blue. Gossamer tendrils of smoke wafted from their settings and curled into the air over Enderfon's head. They smelled peppery. The tendrils thickened quickly into heavy clouds that sank to the Coldside Sea's surface.

The mace pulled Enderfon's trembling arms toward the water. He stumbled as it forced him toward the shoreline until he stood where waves broke over his stony toes. Dark clouds rose from the water, gusts carried them aloft, and in their place sat a causeway, a land bridge stretching from his toes to the edge of the Coldside Sea Island.

Sweetnettle flitted in front of his eyes, wings flapping in a blur. "What's wrong with you? Let's move."

"I can't. My legs."

"You can't walk?"

"No, you'll have to go alone. Some spell has bound my legs to the shore. Use that land bridge to fly, rest, and fly again to reach the island. In the meantime, I'll find a way to free myself. Rowel will help me."

"I won't leave you. Anyway, this fierce wind will carry me away."

Enderfon sighed. "Very well. I suppose you're right. Please sit here then while I sing to Rowel again."

Sweetnettle flew down to the sandy beach and settled in the hollow of a large boulder. Enderfon murmured a lullaby and tucked a crimson coverlet around him with his little finger. The sprite's head nodded and his eyelids drooped. Happy to see his little friend dozing, Enderfon focused on the problem at his feet. He had to undo the enchantment.

Grunting, Enderfon strained to lift one leg. It stuck to the rocky shore. Maybe he had left out something. He sang again. Another failure. He tried a different spell tune but sighed when it did not work. He chanted one more time, filling the air with a soft but powerful spell-breaker.

A dragon's scream pierced Enderfon's song, and he nearly dropped Rowel. A Golden Dragon broke through the clouds with a rider sitting astride its hump.

"Sweetnettle, wake up. Aurykk and Rocánonom are here!"

ROCÁNONOM

THE MOMENT AURYKK'S WINGS cut through the cloud cover, Rocánonom blinked in disbelief. His old friend Enderfon stood on the shore below. "Halloo, brother!" he shouted, but the wind snatched away his words. He urged Aurykk to glide down and hover near the rock giant.

When the Golden was close enough for the giants to hear each other, his wings fluttered and he belched a few globs of sticky cinders. They fell on Enderfon's head.

"Hey," the rock giant cried, rubbing his pate.

"Sorry, Enderfon. I'm surprised you felt that, but I am *delighted* to see you after so many World-Turns. How are you?" Rocánonom laughed.

"If my stony eyes could weep, you'd see tears of joy. Are you well?"

"Couldn't be better."

"Old friend, I am stuck here. I think an Impedimentum spell is binding my legs."

"Not to worry." Rocánonom held out his hand to beckon the sprite. "Hello, Sweetnettle; good to see you, too. Come help me fix this."

With a tinkling giggle, Sweetnettle flew up to Rocánonom's shoulder. He wrapped his legs around the giant's upper arm. "How may I help?"

"Take this string and loop it around Enderfon, then bring your end back to me."

Sweetnettle flew off, circled Enderfon, and returned. Rocánonom tied one end of the string around his waist and gripped the other knotted end in his fist.

"What next?" the Lobli asked.

"Go back to Enderfon. Stay close. If I can remember the words, I shall chant away the Impedimentum and protect both of you." Rocánonom pictured the torn, mold-stained page of the grimoire where he had found the Encirclement spell he'd used to protect himself and Aurykk from the Malevir's detection. Could he spread the spell a bit more? His memory pulled up a small diagram on the page. Under it, someone had written one line—*torra ektinonontay giro apo.* Using his free hand, he followed the string with one finger. The string glittered in response to Rocánonom's chanting.

A cluster of clouds slowly descended over the rock giant and the Lobli. It dissolved into a silvery shower of damp flakes coating them both and absorbing the string.

Sweetnettle brushed off the flakes and flew back to Rocánonom. "His legs are free. He thanks you for the protection. Also, my brother Loblin gave us their black curtain, which will help us approach the island unseen."

"What curtain?"

"Before reaching this shore, Enderfon and I rested a while in Anonom. Your Loblin gave me this."

He pulled a small rolled-up curtain from his pack. Holding it in front of himself, Sweetnettle snapped it three times and disappeared.

"Ho! That's why I didn't see the Lobli when I left the manor house. Clever. They were hiding behind it."

Sweetnettle rolled up the curtain. "They said the Malevir won't see us coming." He swept through the air in a little figure eight and glided back to Enderfon. He settled into the giant's shoulder.

Enderfon looked up at Rocánonom. "Rowel will help us now."

"When you reach the island, what will you do?"

"With Rowel, I can melt the tower's ice walls. Easier to find the Malevir."

"Aurykk and I will take care of him."

"No, wait. Isabella and Draako are sitting outside the tower. I don't see their riders. We must find them first, before an attack on the Malevir."

"Did Nnylf and Alana enter the tower?"

Enderfon shook his head. "I don't know." He waved goodbye and stepped onto the land bridge.

As Enderfon slogged toward the island, Rocánonom wiped his sweaty brow and settled on Aurykk's rider's hump. "Aurykk, would Isabella and Draako let Nnylf and Alana explore the tower without them?"

The Golden shook his head. "Too dangerous for dragons."

"Well, yes, but—"

Aurykk's long neck bent back toward his hump. "You went inside the tower when you last visited it many World-Turns ago. What did you see?"

"Huge rocks. Icy walls covering dark, shadowy things, other rocks, maybe."

"You didn't go further within?"

"No. I was looking for the grimoire. I found it on a block of ice near the door. I took it and fled the island."

"*Hush!*" Aurykk's alarmed thought rattled Rocánonom's head.

"What?"

Aurykk flew straight up into the clouds. Rocánonom listened for the dragon's words. Hearing nothing, he called out, "What are you doing? We can't leave now. This makes no sense. Go back." The

Golden flew on in silence until they were far out over the sea and the island was a dark shadow on the horizon.

"Answer me. Please," Rocánonom begged.

The Golden glided lower and skimmed along the sea's surface. *We're far enough from the Malevir. He can't hear us now, but I'm sure he heard you say you took the grimoire. He'll be waiting for us now, especially for you.*

"He really is in the tower? I wasn't sure."

Yes, in his stronghold.

"Hasn't it always been his tower?"

No. I was about to tell you. The island was, should still be, a dragon burial place. Aurykk sniffed and, with a shiver, he coughed a cloud of cinders. *Before the Malevir used his enchantments to steal it from them, dragons in their Twilight Time went there to die. They turned to stone and lay there for all World-Turns.*

Aurykk looped a figure eight before skimming the water again. Rocánonom's knees quivered, and his arms ached from gripping the Golden's neck frill. He wanted to return to the shore. "Why are you telling me this? The riders are in danger and we mustn't delay."

I fear many dragons are Kurnan's fellow prisoners. Their last agonies will never end. The Malevir wants to trap the rest of us dragons in that tower with any bait he can find. He chose Kurnan to lure us here—perhaps to force you to return the grimoire to him in exchange for Kurnan's freedom—that is, if he knows you have hidden it in my cave. Aurykk cleared his throat with an angry blast of flame.

Rocánonom's heart beat faster. He wondered what he should do. Would the Encirclement spell hide his words from the Malevir? If he called on Elementals to help him, might the Malevir escape? Without a proper grave, would his captive dragon spirits lie in torment, forever wraiths?

"Listen to me, Aurykk. Rowel's power might overcome the Malevir for a while. Enderfon will melt the tower's ice walls and, I hope, free the captive dragons. They will go to their final rest. Then we'll summon the Fire Elemental and attack the Malevir."

Aurykk threw back his head and snorted. *Not so fast. We must wait until the riders are safe. If Enderfon and Rowel succeed, you can call on the Elemental.*

Rocánonom hunkered down as Aurykk headed back to the pebbly beach lining the shore of the Coldside Sea. All the while, questions about the Malevir dogged him. What was the Malevir? Why did he want every dragon in Dragonwolder dead? Surely not for the grimoire alone. What would the Malevir gain from a world with no dragons?

ENDERFON

H E DID NOT NOTICE the Golden's sudden bound skyward until he heard Sweetnettle squeak, "Why did Aurykk fly so high and far away?"

"I don't know, scouting maybe? Where are they now?"

"Flying back to the shore of the Coldside Sea."

Enderfon turned to watch them glide onto the beach. "Good. They're safe. Let's keep going. We have work to do." His long strides brought him halfway across the land bridge.

Sweetnettle fluttered to and from Enderfon's shoulder. He rested a while then flew off. Circling the giant's head once, he chirped, "Like them, I shall scout a bit."

Enderfon shook his head. "I don't think you should—" but Sweetnettle zipped away to the island before the giant could stop him.

"See you soon, my little friend!" Enderfon called as he lost sight of the sprite. Sweetnettle was such a tiny creature. Would he survive the buffeting winds? He trudged on toward the island and spotted his old friends Draako and Isabella pacing the shore. As Enderfon approached them, the Silver bobbed his head, stretched his wings, and leaped into the sky. Enderfon blinked as Draako's thoughts filled his head.

Hurry! Our riders are somewhere in the tower. We couldn't keep them with us. Dragon lore forbids us to enter.

So they are *inside. Did Sweetnettle find you? He's spying on the island.*

Draako dipped and flew around the giant's shoulders. *No sign of him. He would not have entered from here anyway. See, the tower door is now blocked with ice. Probably up by the spires. It's open to the sky.*

If I find the right spell, Rowel will melt that ice blocking the door. Look out for my Lobli friend. I'll join you on the island.

Enderfon watched Draako circle the island then disappear behind the tower's spires. How would Sweetnettle find the strength to fly that high? *I wish he had stayed with me.*

With a shrill cry, the dragon reappeared and swooped toward him. He hovered over the last span of the causeway and said out loud, "Enderfon, I found your Lobli."

Sweetnettle parted some folds in Draako's neck frill, crawled onto one of his spines, and jumped. Fluttering his wings, he flew to Enderfon's shoulder. "Ice seals every tower opening except at the top. I flew into a gap between two spires. Your riders are trapped inside, in cages down on the floor. I heard them calling to each other. The Malevir wasn't around, I guess. Nothing nasty came after me."

Sweetnettle pulled the curtain from his sack and unfurled it. "But just in case the beast is truly in there, we should use this. It will shield us from the Malevir's ears and eyes, if he has any."

Relief flooded through Enderfon. *They're alive!* He still had time to free them. What incantation could move Rowel to send out just enough heat to soften the ice barrier?

He squeezed his eyes shut and waited for the right words to sink into his thoughts. The flutter of Sweetnettle's wings buzzed lightly in his ear. Soon another faint sound covered the first, a low growl that grew louder.

Finally, he heard a voice. *Ah, you have come with Rowel. Eminfoil was right.*

Who speaks?

Lustredust. Rowel's power revived me. Eminfoil trusted you with Rowel. Now you will use her and free me to join my bloodless dam in peace.

Free you?

The Malevir fixed me here in this wall of stone and ice.

Why?

To bring Kurnan and the amulet to him.

Is Kurnan his prisoner?

Yes, but with Rowel you will free us all. You will bring the mace to life with my song.

A cascade of trills, tweedles, and clacks coursed through Enderfon's head. Eventually, they sorted into a droning incantation: *Erif ono emalf, teah oto em,* "fire without flame, bring me heat."

The giant repeated the spell and sang it as quietly as he could. His sides began to itch as the song's words tumbled out of his craggy mouth. Small patches of rock tickled as they slid down his legs. Surely the spell wasn't meant to undo *him*? Ignoring his discomfort, Enderfon chanted the spell again and again. More pebbles and slabs of slate peeled off his tough shell.

Suddenly, Rowel came to life. The mace's gems glowed like a phosphorous sea. Enderfon's painful itching faded away. Gravel and dust settled at his feet, and his body moved with a lightness he had not known for many World-Turns.

Well done, old friend. Once you step onto the island, wave Rowel's head across the frozen rocks. Repeat the spell I gave you.

And?

Lustredust did not answer. Enderfon waited, but no words from the ancient dragon came to him. With a shrug, he hefted Rowel onto his shoulder and strode toward the island. He clambered up its slippery, rocky shore and saw Isabella pacing along its length.

Stones and slush tumbled away from the Copper Dragon's heavy footsteps. Chunks of ice crashed into the rough sea below her path, and colossal waves washed over Enderfon's feet. Isabella looked at Enderfon, and she sat back on her haunches and stretched her wings.

"At last you found us!" Isabella looked him up and down. "What happened to your body? It's much…I don't know…smoother?"

"Lighter. The spell I used to bring Rowel to life sloughed off some of my stone shell."

With a whoosh of frigid air, Draako landed next to Isabella. He said, "Enderfon, I'm glad you're here. Not a moment too soon. We cannot hear our riders' thoughts. We don't know what happened to them."

"May the Ways of the World protect them," Isabella wailed. Her eyes were turning a dangerous scarlet. Enderfon knew he had to calm her. He raised Rowel and pointed it just above her. A shower of glistening dust coated her head and neck. Isabella's eyes glowed amber. She sighed and folded her wings.

"We will find them, Isabella."

Enderfon turned his attention to Sweetnettle. The Lobli was fidgeting on his shoulder. Shifting his sack to the small of his back he said, "Enderfon, I want to spy from the tower spires again."

"No, stay here with me. Rowel's ready."

Enderfon stroked the mace head. The gems were warm and brilliant. *I can't wait any longer to use Rowel. The young riders might die.* He pointed the mace toward the island's center. The magical black curtain protecting him and Sweetnettle floated in the air between him and the tower and faded to a thin line of black thread around its edges. Enderfon looked through it. He pointed Rowel at the tower's iced-over entrance. "*Erif ono emalf, teah oto em,*" he sang. Gleaming rivulets of melting ice began to flow toward the shore.

ALANA

THE HEAT WAS UNBEARABLE. To fight it, Alana lay on the frozen seawater floor. She pulled her armor over her head and threw the heavy leather tunic across the cage. It hit the glowing bars, and its layered armor plates sizzled. Black smoke surrounded her. She coughed, groaned, and coughed again. The smell of burning leather nauseated her.

Nnylf crawled to the bars and, with a jerk, freed her armor. Smoking bits of shredded and seared leather stuck to the bars.

"Alana, put this on again. You'll need it when they free us."

She looked at the shriveled edges of her ragged armor and grumbled, "Nnylf, no one will free us. We're the Malevir's prisoners. If they could help us, we'd have heard from our dragons."

"Don't give up, not now."

"Draako didn't call you after we entered the tower, did he?"

"No, but he must have gone for help. And Enderfon might be here soon."

"Enderfon? I doubt it. He was going to meet us here, but even if he made it to this wretched island, what could he do?"

"They'll figure it out." Nnylf tugged at her armor and raised her chin with one finger. "There, it's still useful. How does it feel?"

"Warm." Alana avoided meeting his eyes. She crawled to the side of the cage that faced Kurnan. "Brother, can you hear me?" Her voice echoed from the walls. Kurnan's answer overlapped her words.

"Yes, yes."

"Can you see what's happening?"

She barely heard his hoarse reply. "Weird, the floor's shifting under my feet. Same for you?"

She looked around the cage. Its bars were sinking into the floor. She teetered as the floor wobbled, and her feet started to slide toward the glowing bars. She grabbed Nnylf's arm. "Help me, Nnylf!" she screamed. "Hang on, Kurnan, and dig into the ice."

Nnylf's feet slipped, but he held onto his small ax, wedged deep in slushy ice. With her free hand, Alana rummaged in her sack and found her own ax. She stabbed it into the floor and hung onto the handle. Nnylf was gripping her arm as tightly as she held onto his. Where was her brother in this mess?

"Kurnan!" she screamed. "Talk to me."

When her echoing cries faded, she heard her brother's faint answer: "I see something. A light. The ice is melting. I..." His last word hung in the air.

"Kurnan, answer me!" she screamed.

"Alana, my arm, so tired!" Nnylf shouted. "Shaking. Let's call our dragons again."

"What's the use? The Malevir—" She bit back her despair when she saw disappointment flicker in Nnylf's eyes, replacing his usual warmth and affection. His look boosted her courage. She examined her grimy fingers, numb with cold, and wrapped them more tightly around the ax handle. She had to try. Maybe, now that the wall had opened a bit, Isabella would hear her.

Gasping as the floor tilted again, she shouted, "Right! I'm trying!" and squeezed his arm. She forced a tight smile. "You, too?"

Nnylf nodded and closed his eyes.

With her eyes shut, Alana pictured Isabella's beautiful head dipping in and out of the clouds. *Answer me, my beautiful friend, my Copper. We're in terrible danger.*

Isabella did not answer. Alana glanced up. The cage's roof was lower than before. If it fell, it would crush and burn her and Nnylf. Was Kurnan's cage doing the same? Her head whirled, and she shouted, "Kurnan, call Isabella! Try hard. Tell her you're in here. Tell her you need her."

Kurnan did not answer. She called again. Her breath caught in her throat. Was he dead?

"Kurnan, answer me."

She heard only the creak of breaking ice and Nnylf's struggling breaths. After too long a silence, her brother's words seemed to slide across the ice floor. "Quiet. Please stop talking. I hear her now. I do, I hear my Isabella!"

At that moment, a wave of cuttingly cold water cascaded over her and Nnylf. The whole cage turned on its side, and clouds of steam filled the air. Alana's hand slipped, and she lost her grip on Nnylf's arm. The water swelled and carried her across the floor, out the widening door of the tower. Fighting to keep her head above water, Alana gulped for air as a whirlpool sucked her in.

Darkness enveloped Alana as she sank into the bitterly cold water. She didn't remember breathing until a wave tossed her onto snow-covered rocks. She wiped her eyes and stared. A bedraggled stranger lay next to her, at the feet of her dragon. Under his thatch of filthy hair, startled eyes returned her gaze.

KURNAN

He called out to Alana as his prison cage upended. Sliding under the pronged ends of its steaming bars, Kurnan thrashed, searching for a handhold. When a thunderous torrent carried him away from the collapsing cage, he regretted never learning to swim. Like a dog, he pawed through the water. It whirled him around, but he kept his head above the surface.

Kurnan swallowed water. He coughed it out. He breathed in another mouthful; it burned his throat and his chest ached. His legs kicked furiously until another huge wave flipped them into the air and tossed Kurnan onto a rock. His head hit it hard.

When Kurnan opened his eyes, he found himself in a shallow pool of icy water. At least he could breathe. A woman was shaking him.

He shook his head. Muffled sounds sharpened as water trickled out of his clogged ears.

"Kurnan, Kurnan. Thank the Ways of the World. Do you know me?"

He studied the woman's face. She was young—and pretty despite the soggy tresses draped across her head. Of course he knew her. "Alana? You *were* in there. I wasn't dreaming, right? You're not another of the Malevir's tricks?" The sight of his sister filled him with such warmth he nearly forgot his shivering.

Alana stroked his hair and rinsed the small wound on his forehead with sea water.

"Ouch!"

"Washing off the dirt. Oh, Kurnan, you're not angry with me, are you?"

"Why should I be? No, I am so very happy to see you." Kurnan smiled at his sister. She cradled his head and kissed his cheek.

A gust of warm air brushed Kurnan's body. He looked up. Isabella's long neck swayed over him and Alana. His Copper. This was no dream. He could hear her thoughts.

Kurnan, you live! Hurry, climb up before you drown. The tower's collapsing.

Kurnan looked back at his former prison. Great boulders and cut stones were tumbling from the tower spires. Ice walls once holding them in place had become a rushing, deadly stream.

"Was that Nnylf with you? Where is he?"

"Draako and Nnylf flew to the seashore!" Alana screamed above the screeching wind.

"Yes!" Isabella's shrill call pierced the chaos surrounding them. "Now we, too, must fly before it's too late."

The happiness coursing through Kurnan's body confused him. Where were the anger and spite that had driven him with mad strength across the Warmside and into the Meeting of Mountains? Despite Isabella's pleas and Alana's help, Kurnan could not persuade his legs to stand. The voices had pushed him throughout Dragonwolder but, like their powerful amulet, they had deceived him and stolen his will. Without them, he was weak.

Isabella grabbed him, and Kurnan's feet left the ground. His head jerked back as he landed in front of Alana on the rider's hump. "Ouf!" he yelped at the fleeting pain.

Alana hugged him tightly. "Don't worry. I've got you. Do you remember how to grip with your knees?"

A memory flashed: Lustredust's powerful leap through the cavern's roof and the moment he'd reconnected to a dragon's ways. Yes, yes, he did know how to grip with his knees, but what had happened to Lustredust?

ENDERFON

A JUMBLE OF ROCKS AND boulders surrounded the last structure still standing on the island. Billowing grit floated overhead. Enderfon coughed as sulfurous steam hissed from the glowing branches of a colossal tree at the heart of the tower's ruins. The tree extended far above his head. He guessed its topmost branches had supported the tower's spires before the frozen heights melted away. The glare of the blue-black branches stung his eyes.

Shouldering Rowel, he picked his way across the rocks and stopped where the tower's door had once stood. Beyond the threshold, a slew of dragon bodies sprawled across huge crescent-shaped boulders, rising from the sea. The dragons lay knotted in private agonies. Enderfon could hear their weak groans and whimpers. Beyond them another dragon, with fading golden scales, sat on his haunches. His head swayed slowly side to side.

Enderfon circled the cluster of dragons. Their faded colors and limp bodies made them look more dead than alive. As if the Golden had read Enderfon's thoughts, he said, *We might as well be dead, but the Malevir denies us our proper rest.*

"Who speaks?"

You know me as Lustredust. Free me.

"You honor me, great one, but how? You gave me Rowel. Will her powers help you?"

No. Fire is required. Lustredust sank to his knees. His head lay sideways in the dust, and he closed his eyes.

"Lustredust, I have no fire. What must I do?"

The Golden's slack mouth sagged, and his tongue lay across his fangs. His silence stirred unfamiliar panic in Enderfon's chest. He searched his memory for some forgotten spell he might once have known.

A tug on his earlobe startled Enderfon.

Sweetnettle flew onto his nose. "Lustredust's spirit joins those sad dragon wraiths below. For countless World-Turns, he was the Malevir's slave. But look, Rocánonom and Aurykk are coming. They will finish our work and free Lustredust. He will find his eternal rest."

Enderfon held out his hand, now softening into folds of crackling skin. The Lobli floated onto his palm and sat cross-legged. "Enderfon, do you see what's happening to you?"

"Oh, well, I've shed some weight recently."

"More than that. Your body is changing in bits and pieces."

"You're right. It started with Rowel's magic song."

"Are you still strong? Let's cross back over the land bridge."

"Not yet." Enderfon pointed to the dragon wraiths. "We cannot leave them. They need our help here."

"No, when we leave and are safely away, Rocánonom and Aurykk will do what is needed."

Enderfon's spell had melted the tower but almost drowned his friends. Sadness and foreboding pumped through him, and his heart, once buried so deep in his rock-bound body, ached to help them. Shouldn't he protect these dragons from the Malevir? He did not wish them more torment. "Did I drown our young riders and their dragons?"

"No, no. They all escaped. Look, Aurykk and Rocánonom are overhead!"

"But, Kurnan?"

"He flew away with Alana and Isabella."

Enderfon's face flushed with unfamiliar, but soothing, warmth. "Good. I won't insist any longer. Let's go." He sighed. "May the Ways of the World give Rocánonom and Aurykk wisdom and strength to help these poor dragon spirits. Rowel, awaken and give me strength too." The mace's gems glowed and surrounded the giant in a honey-colored aura. As soon as his rough, stony shell felt the light's heat, it cracked again and shed more stones and gravel.

Enderfon shifted the mace from one hand to the other as he stared at his arms and legs in awe. Small patches of tawny skin had appeared where, before, rocks and stones had covered his bulky limbs. With a lighter step, he returned to the causeway and headed toward the opposite shore. *Now, Malevir, now, you will meet your match.*

ROCÁNONOM

Aurykk's wingbeats slowed. Rocánonom squeezed his knees against the rider's hump as his dragon friend dipped sharply toward the island. They hovered high above the top of a towering dark tree. Its trunk and branches pulsed with a sickly blue light. Wispy bodies resembling dragons writhed at its base. They quivered and twitched in a shallow pool of the seawater washing over the island.

"Rowel," the giant muttered to himself.

He heard Aurykk's inner voice. *Yes, Rowel. Only the Mystic Scintilla's power could thaw that tower.*

"True, true, but those bodies down there, who are they?"

Ancestors of dragonkin, freed from the melted tower walls but still the Malevir's captives.

"And the tree?"

My inner light sees only death and decay.

"Perhaps it's time to—"

Quiet. Aurykk bobbed his head and circled higher. Rocánonom clung to the dragon's frill as they soared up, out of the Malevir's earshot.

When Rocánonom was sure they were far from the Malevir's detection, he drew in a deep breath and wiped the nervous sweat from his forehead. He knew his enemy's magick could find him, but the spell protecting him and the Golden distorted the Malevir's view of their flight.

"My friend, hold steady. I'm preparing to call the Fire Elemental!" Rocánonom shouted. He fished through his sack for a length of twine. "With your permission, I'll tie myself to your spines, the ones just behind me, so I won't fall when my legs are slack."

Do that, and use the long spines by my ears too, if you wish.

"I would if I could reach that far." Rocánonom set about securing himself to the dragon. As he tightened the last knot, a gnarled branch of the tree shot up and wrapped its tendrils around Aurykk's rear leg. The Golden screeched. He belched a few cinders and let fly a wave of flame. The seared branch twisted and turned black. It crumbled, and its ashes settled on the dragon wraiths below.

Aurykk flew higher still. Rocánonom hoped they were well beyond the tree's reach. Without another glance downward, he closed his eyes and clutched Aurykk's frill. His breathing slowed, and he plunged into the darkness behind his eyelids. Little sparks darted across deepening emptiness as he fell into a trance.

Rocánonom saw himself surrounded by nightmarish fire, burning ever hotter, hissing and crackling. He imagined pulling the false fire inside his body. Hot and dense, it formed a ball in his stomach. It did not burn. Eyes clamped shut, he raised his arms and sang out the grimoire's archaic enchantment:

> Fyreburn, by the power at my command
> from The Most Ancient Book of Spells,
> and summoning with a pure heart, I call you.
> Come, Fyreburn, with your searing white light born in
> earth's core.

Grant me the power to let you fly.

Let your flames ring our enemy, the Destroyer, the Malevir, until he boils.

Rocánonom waited. The fireball throbbed in his belly, neither shrinking nor growing. His legs floated away from Aurykk's sides. Icy ribbons of fear ran down his arms, but he would not lose his grip on Aurykk's frill.

ROCÁNONOM!

His eyes snapped open. A whirlwind surrounded him and Aurykk. Grit and ashes stung his face and hands. *A firestorm. It could eat us alive.* His empty stomach churned. He licked his dry lips, and his tongue felt like parched grass.

The swirling smoke and ashes parted. Four columns of fire rose out of the smoke. Each column twisted and turned until it looked like a salamander made of embers and blazing plumes. All four towered over him and Aurykk, their scarlet eyes awash in a field of black. The lizards circled him. They grew. They took the form of immense red and yellow dragons. Their wings and crests snapped like angry flames in a damp hearth.

Master, you command.

A cloud of sulfurous fumes ringed Rocánonom and Aurykk. Rocánonom coughed and his throat burned. Aurykk had no such problem. His flesh rippled as he reared up to face the Elementals and he called, *Answer them! Hurry!*

"Fyreburn, your kin lie in agony below. Redeem them."

Master, command us.

How could he command these creatures? Now that the moment was here, he could not imagine what he should say. Rocánonom gasped and tears welled in his eyes.

They will sniff out the beast, Aurykk said. *Answer them. Tell them to attack.*

Rocánonom's belly knotted and he gasped. "Aurykk, you're right. Wherever the Malevir hides, the Elementals will find him. They must find him." He swiveled his gaze to meet the smoldering eyes of each dragon. "Fyreburn!" he shouted. "Please use your great force to drive the Malevir from this place. Ring him with your flames until he boils."

The Fire Elementals hung in the air, like smoke rising up a chimney but motionless. Rocánonom coughed again. He spat bits of cinder and ash and picked them from his tongue.

Rocánonom, don't ask them. Command them.

Rocánonom let one of his hands loosen its hold on Aurykk's frill. He raised his aching right arm and screamed, "Fyreburn, obey me, by the power of The Most Ancient Book of Spells! I command you to find the Malevir and destroy him!"

Each dragon returned Rocánonom's gaze with a dark and steady glare. He could feel their heat as they tightened their circle around him and Aurykk. Sweat pooled under his tunic, in the hollows of his neck, and in his armpits. A pearly haze filled the space between him and the Elementals.

Rocánonom jerked back as Aurykk jolted upward, away from the Elementals. Or were the fiery spirits sinking? Their smoky circle lay below. As Aurykk rose up and up, Rocánonom tasted clean, cold air.

They're circling the tree!

Aurykk's call shook Rocánonom from his brief reverie. He looked down. Heat waves shimmered around the dark tree. Its branches thrashed like the arms of someone drowning in the Coldside Sea.

Each Elemental blasted the tree with otherworldly flames, whirling around it in a firestorm of destruction. Billows of green and purple clouds blanketed the tree and settled on the dragon wraiths at its base. All of them—the tree, the wraiths, and the Elementals—disappeared in thick smoke.

Far above the chaos, Aurykk glided back and forth. The clouds lingered below. Anxious to see the results of the Elementals' magic,

Rocánonom urged Aurykk to fly closer to them. Never, in Rocánonom's memory, had the world seemed to turn so slowly.

An anguished roar broke through the clouds. The Elementals vanished. The clouds broke apart and drifted away. Crumpled and motionless bodies of dragon wraiths no longer ringed the black tree's base. Rocánonom urged Aurykk to land. He so wanted to find them, to help them. The Golden did not answer but pointed to the hideous tree.

A charred shell of its former self, the tree quivered and swayed. With a thunderous crack, its shell collapsed into miniscule sooty bits before rising to float above the island. The bits whirled and came together, like a murmuration of blackbirds, into the shape of an enormous blue-black dragon. The creature sped toward the dark orb, masking one edge of the sun. It plunged into the orb, which then shrank until it blinked out of sight.

Where the tree once stood, dragon footprints trailed across the pebble-covered platform and led toward the sea. Rocánonom shared his thoughts with Aurykk. *The dragon spirits' instincts return them to the sea.*

Yes, where all our kind yearn to be at the end of our days.

The edge of a small object, glowing in the brightening sun, caught Rocánonom's eye. "Aurykk, the Malevir left behind one of his trinkets, over there outside the walls of the tower."

"Hang on. I'm going to snatch it and store it in my jaw pouch."

"No. Not if it's what I think it is. Let it be." He tugged at Aurykk's neck frill as the dragon swooped across the rocky platform toward the object. Aurykk kicked it. The object landed between two large rocks at the sea's edge.

DRAAKO

He left Nnylf on the shore of the Coldside Sea and returned to the island. Draako was not prepared for the howling fire-storm that greeted him. He shot up into the sky far above the chaos and called to Aurykk and Rocánonom, darting back and forth below him. They did not answer.

Rocánonom was commanding Fire Elementals, whose flames engulfed a grotesque, gigantic tree where the ice tower once stood. The Elementals soon joined tails and spun into a whirlwind before fading away. Aurykk and Rocánonom spiraled down to the billows of smoke rising from the dying flames.

Draako soared higher and circled the island. He dodged strong winds blowing away the smoke. His heart jumped when an enormous blue-black dragon rose from the island's center. Draako blinked his eyes. Were they tricking him? Was the dragon an illusion, a trail of smoke escaping from the crumbling ruins? When the specter reached the dark orb, both vanished and the sun grew brighter.

Below Draako lay the shadowy bodies of dragon wraiths, curled like crisp autumn leaves around the tree's base. They rose and shuffled to the shore. One by one, they plunged into the sea and disappeared into the surging waves. He took a deep breath and blew out the mass of cinders clogging his tightened throat.

Draako circled the island one last time. The wraiths were free of the beast or they would not have plunged into the sea. Was the strange dark dragon yet another creature of the Malevir, shifted into a new shape, or had he been looking at the beast's true self? Draako had no way of knowing. He needed to touch down on the island and look at the tower ruins for himself. His spark glands swelled with his urge to know what had happened there. He yearned to enter the former stronghold's grounds.

He wanted to ask Aurykk if he should explore the ruins, but he did not see the Golden nor Rocánonom anywhere near the island. He sent his uncle his thoughts, but Aurykk did not answer. *He must be checking on the others.* Draako winged a few more loops away from the island. Out on the land bridge, he spotted Enderfon, but his curiosity pulled him away from his giant friend and back to the island.

Draako's back legs landed first, and his wings flapped hard to lift him off the still-scorching rocks and gravel that lay where the blue-black tree had stood. He skimmed along the sea to cool his feet. Approaching shore, he spotted the cluster of rocks where he and Isabella had waited for their riders when they were trapped in the tower. With a sigh of relief, Draako settled onto the cool rocks and sat back on his haunches. He looked around. *I could sit here for a while, until the base of the tower cools a bit.* He eased his belly onto the rocks and, stretching his forelegs in front of him, he sniffed the rocks.

A bitter smell filled Draako's nostrils. Many World-Turns ago, he had breathed in that same unpleasant scent. The amulet! That was the smell of the amulet he had found in the aiglonax's ashes after the Valley folk and dragon flokks destroyed the beast. His nostrils widened as he turned his head to find the source of the biting stink.

Lying between two rocks, a crumpled piece of metal claimed his attention. He crept closer to it. The reek grew stronger and Draako gagged. He cleared his throat with a blast of white smoke and lowered his head to see the object more closely. It did resemble the disk-shaped amulet he knew, the one he'd discovered in Aindle's ashes, the one responsible for Kurnan's illness and journey far from Fossarelick. In its sorry state, like a battered shell, it lay jammed between the rocks, destined to disappear in the eternal pounding of sea waves.

Draako's claws wrapped around the object and yanked it free. Each side had some writing, partially hidden by gouges and scorch marks. Draako picked out the runes for "dust" on one side, the last part of his ghost relative's name.

On the other side, he easily read, "One and only One will dare to banish pain and fear." Fire had erased the rider's name. Draako was sure it would have read "Aindle." He remembered Aurykk's explanation: the Malevir, disguised as Aindle, a dragonrider, had ridden Lustredust and worn the amulet. He was the rider who murdered Lustredust's dam, Eminfoil, and drove the ancient Golden to kill himself. Aindle then transformed into an ogre-like hork before shifting into the fearsome aiglonax that attacked Dragonwolder.

Draako brushed the splotches of grit and soot off the disk with a careful claw. He blasted it with flames and cleaned it with seawater until it no longer reeked.

Draako's clan, the Orferans, had long considered him the One and only One. They expected him to be the one leader who, for all times, would banish pain and fear. They called him the Rightful Reader, the dragon who had fulfilled a prophecy carved over the entrance to the Cave of the Ancestors. If so, then this relic of an old menace, this worthless mangled amulet, rightfully would be his to keep, a souvenir of a vanquished enemy. He stashed the disk in his jaw pouch, licked his fangs, and flew back to his companions.

ENDERFON

HE STOOD HALFWAY ACROSS the land bridge. Sweetnettle's wings tickled Enderfon's nose, and he raised his hand to chase away the sprite. He stopped. That hand did not look like his own. Enderfon steadied Rowel between his thighs and rubbed one hand with the other. They were warm. He raised them again and examined each of his now supple fingers. He could wiggle them. Reddish-tan flesh, not stones, covered them.

Puzzled, Enderfon scratched the top of his head. His newly sensitive fingers found soft hair where jutting rocks used to sit. Hair! He'd forgotten the short black curls that had covered his head so many World-Turns ago.

Sweetnettle buzzed in his ear, "I like your face now, without all those rough pebbles. Reminds me of Rocánonom's, but you're..."

"I'm what?"

"Taller and, er—ah-hem." Sweetnettle was blushing deep green as he circled the giant's torso.

"Something wrong?"

"Your tunic."

Enderfon looked down. His mouth hung open, and he choked at the sight of another surprise. Whose belly was that? Gone, the sharp, rocky edges. Crumbled away, his cold and gritty crust. He hesitated then swept his palm across his smooth chest. His skin itched, and he scratched it. A few remaining pebbles fell away. *That was satisfying.* A brisk, cold wind sweeping across the sea brushed his new skin. It made him shiver, but he liked feeling the chill.

"You might want to cover up," Sweetnettle whispered in his ear and pointed to the goose bumps spreading across Enderfon's naked body. "Use the curtain for now." The Lobli whirled a finger in the air. The magic curtain that had protected them from the Malevir materialized. It draped itself around Enderfon from his armpits to his knees.

Sweetnettle wriggled into the giant's shoulder. "What will you do now with Rowel?"

Tucking the curtain snugly around his middle, Enderfon winked and grasped the mace in his right hand. "Remember when you found me at the edge of the Warmside Beyond?"

"You picked up Rowel and pointed her at the ground."

Enderfon pointed it at the devastated island. "And her light turned hard rock into soil."

"Can she do it again?"

"I will try." Enderfon called to his mace, "Rowel, hear my song and do your best. Life, return to the island. Dragons find your rest."

Enderfon hummed the one melody he knew would awaken Rowel's magick. The wordless song rose and fell on eight notes. Once more, as at the red needlerock, the tune came from deep in his throat. The air thrummed around him and Sweetnettle.

Rowel's gems gleamed. Emeralds and sapphires pulsed beams of green and blue-white light toward the island. Enderfon raised the mace head and aimed its beams at the tower ruins. Rocks strewn across its melted floor brightened. *Lustredust, are you there? Can you feel Rowel's warm light?* His eyes ached, and his arm was tiring. He called the Lobli. "Sweetnettle, Lustredust does not answer me. Fly over the island. Tell me what you see, but do not fly inside Rowel's beams."

Without a word, Sweetnettle raced away. Enderfon watched him soar above the calm sea waters until he reached a cluster of rocks steaming in the heat of the mace's beams. *Time to finish the job.* He sang again to Rowel:

> The heart of good magic beats in you.
> Heeding your powers, life springs anew.
> Go gentle now and let them rise,
> The dragons and gardens to fill my eyes.

Rowel's light beams dimmed until they left only a shimmer in the air over the island. Steam turned to rain, bathing the island with a downpour. A stiff breeze scattered the remaining clouds and they drifted out to sea.

Enderfon called to Sweetnettle. *What do you see?*

Marvels and wonders. If nowhere else in Dragonwolder, the Warm-Turn surely is here.

Tell me more.

No more rough rocks and pebbles, except surrounding the shore. Wet brown soil covers every patch of ground touched by the light. Green sprouts are poking through the earth and uncurling toward the sun. Oh, the sun! Look!

A spasm jolted Enderfon's neck as he turned too quickly. Where was the sun's pale self? A round golden star sat overhead in a brightening sky. Enderfon could feel its growing warmth tug at the scales and gravel still clinging to his skin.

What of the dragons?

I see them. They sleep beneath the waves lapping the shore.

Lustredust sleeps with them?

The great Golden lies next to his dam, Eminfoil. Like the other dragons, they are colossal rocks.

I must see them.

Enderfon strode back to the island. When he reached the end of the bridge, he saw a breakwater of big rocks curled like sleeping dragons. Not daring to step on them, he called out, "Dragon spirits, let me hear you."

As if from a distance, a chorus of voices answered Enderfon.

Thank you.

Welcome.

You, great one, may walk upon us.

Enderfon bowed, hesitating at first, then stepped onto the closest dragon rock. He jumped as a voice greeted him. *Ha! I thought you'd be heavier.*

Who speaks?

Drakeana.

Enderfon's heart leaped. The voice belonged to a dragon he had once known. *Worthy dam and ancestor of the Orferans, how fare you now?*

Well. My voice will fade soon as the Great Sleep enfolds me, but we--yawn--thank you. Our hearts are stone, but our spirits beat in peace. We dragon spirits now lie around the island. We savor our perfect end.

May the Ways of the World give you endless peace.

With Drakeana's faint farewell, Enderfon crossed her broad, flat flank and stepped onto the island. Sweetnettle landed on his shoulder with a soft bounce. The giant climbed the steep slope up to the tower ruins. Catching his breath, Enderfon gasped then smiled. "Sweetnettle, the ghostly tree is gone, *and* a garden has taken its place."

The Lobli fluttered to the ground and plucked a leaf from a spreading patch of green shoots. "Umm..." He crushed a leaf in his hand. "Smells herby, and over there, do you see my namesake plant, sweet nettle? Its little purple flowers soon will cover the ground."

"The island looks soft and leafy, as the dragons would have wanted, a quiet green space to guard their Great Sleep."

"Yes. Our living dragon friends will rest here too, without fear, at the end of their days."

Sweetnettle flew little circles in front of Enderfon's nose. "Where do we go now?"

Uncrossing his eyes, Enderfon replied, "I see Aurykk and Rocánonom flying this way. I advise you to follow Rocánonom to his tower. He misses you, and I've much work to do in the Coldside Desert. With the Malevir far from Dragonwolder, the UrLoblin finally are free to leave the underearth and return to their desert home. I will help them tame the land and rebuild. I hope to find my friend Haldoren's remains there too. He needs a proper burial."

Sweetnettle patted the giant's cheek. Enderfon's large brown eyes teared at his soft touch. "Fare you well in the coming World-Turn. I hope to see you again, little one."

"Before the next Cold-Turn?"

"Perhaps, Sweetnettle. If the Malevir has truly left us..."

Enderfon scanned the clearing sky above them. Looking past the sun, he whispered, "What if the dark orb returns?"

With a gravelly roar, Aurykk landed and greeted them. Rocánonom slid down the Golden's foreleg and embraced his brother-in-kind.

"How good it is to see you again, like this."

KURNAN

WELL BEFORE ROCÁNONOM AND Enderfon met again, Kurnan was gaping at the Coldside Sea Island. A great fire was sweeping over the island. His sister and his old friend Nnylf stood beside him, and Aurykk was soaring high above the flames. Kurnan's will to fight and outwit the Malevir struggled with his stronger need to survive the beast. Should he run and hide somewhere? He looked for shelter.

His companions gasped at the firestorm. What would become of the island? The tower's collapse boomed across the sea, and gigantic waves crashed against the shore. Isabella and Draako growled and moaned as the fires grew and dark clouds covered the land.

"The dragon spirits..." Isabella keened. "Ways of the World, we must help them."

Draako leaped from the shore with a powerful flap of his wings and skimmed the sea's surface, dotted with whitecaps. "I must go there, to see what has happened," he rumbled to his cousin.

"Go, but take care. Don't touch anything." Isabella ran to the shoreline and watched him fly away toward the island. Standing beside her, Kurnan pressed his hands to his chest. His heart was racing.

He turned toward the roar of the river, Dragonwolder's only major Sunsetside watercourse. Fed by melting snow, it pressed at its banks as it flowed to the Coldside Sea. Kurnan scanned the land he had crossed during the last few Moon-Risings and recalled his confusion and despair at the sight of ice floes on that same river. What madness had brought him here in those days? He yanked his leg from the mud squishing between his toes. His foot popped out of the muck with a loud sucking noise, as if the ground were smacking its lips. *Land of my ancestors, don't swallow me now.*

Upstream from where he and his friends were standing, a plume of steam rose from a crack along the riverbank. The crack soon widened into a large hole. The sound of tinkling giggles filled the air. Where had he heard that? Kurnan trembled. *In the cave, from the creatures that bound me, making me defenseless against uprooters!*

A dainty three-fingered hand with a long slender thumb gripped the hole's rough edge. Kurnan's thoughts were jumbled. *What are they?* More hands clutched the edge of the hole, and a band of Loblin—much bigger than any he had ever known—emerged. When their feet touched the riverbank, they smiled and ran toward him.

Alana and Nnylf dashed past him and embraced the short green sprites. "Kurnan, come meet the UrLoblin," Alana said.

Kurnan's breath came in short gasps. *How could she ask me to do that? They hurt me.* Alana was shaking him now. He whirled around to face her. She was shouting something, her mouth repeating the same shapes. Why couldn't he make sense of her words? "No, wait. Stop, I can't—"

His feet left the ground. He was rising away from his sister, up in the air over the river. Claws held him aloft. Dragon claws.

Kurnan, don't let your painful memories rule you. These little creatures are friends.

A strange word floated into his thoughts, a word he had not used in a long time. "Friends," he whispered. He glanced at the UrLoblin below and repeated the word. Then he croaked, "UrLoblin. Are we friends?"

"Yes, of course you are!" Alana shouted, standing far below them. "We sent them into the cave to find you. They tried to keep you safe."

The Copper drifted slowly down to the riverbank with her eye on Kurnan. She shook her head. "They tried to help, but Lustredust's ghost carried you away."

Nnylf and Alana pulled Kurnan out of his dragon's gentle grip. He tried to stand, but his weak legs buckled, and he fell to his knees. "I am so sorry, so very sorry."

The UrLoblin surrounded him and began to sing a soft melody that reminded Kurnan of his parents' cottage and a pot of stew bubbling on the hearth. He looked down into the sprites' sweet green- and brown-dappled faces and smiled. "Thank you for trying."

Kurnan's vision cleared. He could hear Isabella. Her voice rang out like crystal bells. "Kurnan, sing with them. Let them free you from your past."

Kurnan's head filled with new words:

> Malevir done,
> Rivelam undone.
> Kurnan rebels
> Unravels the spells.
> My new life begun,
> Old life farewell.

Isabella joined him as he repeated the words. The UrLoblin hugged each other and began to giggle.

"You are indeed friends with these UrLoblin, some of the oldest, truest denizens of Dragonwolder," Isabella said.

The UrLoblin patted Kurnan's hands and introduced themselves. They explained their purpose. "We've come to thank you for freeing us. When the Malevir is gone, we shall return to our own home in the Coldside Desert."

"We wish you well," Alana declared.

Before Kurnan could add to his sister's kind remark, Draako returned from his flight over the island and landed with a thud. "Excuse my clumsy landing, please. My feet are a bit scorched. Anyway..." He whooped. "The dragon ancestors are free! I saw the Malevir vanish from Dragonwolder in the orb. A blue-black cloud shaped like a dragon."

Kurnan ran to Draako's side. The UrLoblin cheered and raced back to the hole. They giggled again, waved goodbye, and disappeared into their tunnel network. Within moments the hole closed, and the riverbank resumed its usual shape.

Kurnan needed to see the island for himself. Soft mist enveloped it, and a giant, the one who had helped save him, stood at the other end of the land bridge on the island's shore. He asked Draako, "Why is your giant friend out there? The island is such a terrible place."

"No more. You can see Rowel's magic bathes the island in warm light—berry bushes and tall grass hide the tower's base. The mace's connection to the Mystic Scintilla has restored life to the island where once the icy, barren tower stood.

"I'm sure the dragon spirits have joined their ancestors with great pleasure and relief, as great barrier rocks surrounding the island," Draako continued. "All dragons, including Lustredust, will end their twilight years there. Even I will spend my everlasting rest there."

"Not for a long time, right? Oh look, there's another Golden!" Kurnan wished his thoughts connected better to each other. He'd have one thought, like "Alana, shouldn't we go home now?" but another thought would crowd out the first one—"My stomach's growling"—and he'd forget his first thought. He rubbed his legs, aching with weariness. Lustredust's last words echoed in Kurnan's thoughts.

He both feared and admired the dragon wraith who had rescued him, but he was happy knowing that mysterious Golden was free of the Malevir and at peace. Kurnan relished memories of their flight above the tower, the rediscovered thrill of riding behind a dragon's frill—moments he'd never forget.

"What about *my* frill? Not fancy enough for you?"

Kurnan's cheeks heated up as Isabella's voice interrupted his thoughts. "Nonsense." He laughed. "Without your friendship, my life would have been so...so...ordinary."

"Without your friendship, my grief would be endless. Do you want to go home now? Fly home...with me?"

Alana's "yes!" echoed his own. Kurnan grabbed his sister's wrist and pulled her toward Isabella.

Nnylf was soon at their side. He wrapped one arm around Alana's shoulders and his other around Kurnan. "My friends, all of Dragonwolder will breathe more easily after today. We and our dragons followed the Malevir across Dragonwolder and, with the help of two powerful giants, our dragon friends, and Loblin of all kinds, we have vanquished the beast. The Veiled Valley's Warm-Turn is upon us again, and we've much to do."

With Kurnan and Alana once more seated on her rider's hump, Isabella crouched, spread her wings, and flew in slow beats toward the crest of the Sunsetside Mountains. Draako followed for a short while before pulling away toward the Protectors' Lodge. Kurnan heard him share thoughts with Nnylf.

My friend, the giants believe the Malevir's chilling orb might return. The beast wants our Mystic Scintilla, and we stand in his way. His efforts nearly destroyed us before. He will attack again.

Kurnan shivered as he wrapped his arms around Alana's waist. His knees pressed Isabella's flanks with confidence, but his stomach still churned at the thought of facing his old enemy again. With his friends' help, maybe next time he would be stronger. For now, he had to return to Fossarelick.

What if his family and friends wouldn't welcome him? But surely

Isabella and Alana would make it all turn out well. Wouldn't they? He tightened his jaw as he mentally composed a long list of apologies he had to make and tasks he needed to take up. Going home would not be as easy as riding Isabella, but Kurnan could hardly wait to get there.

EPILOGUE

ONE MOON-RISING LATER, ON a warm, sunny day in the clearing near the Protectors' Lodge. The Copper Dragon and Alana are sitting near each other on the greensward.

"Tell me how it went, with your parents, I mean."

"Well, at first, my parents didn't know what to do or say to Kurnan, but they soon realized he'd changed. He'd learned to overcome his troubles on his long journey. Back home, he raced across the field with new strength, kissed Mother, and gave Father a giant hug. You should have seen how happy they were to see him again."

"We will all need that kind of strength and determination to face the future," Isabella says.

"I don't understand. The Warm-Turn is nearly upon us, we saw the tower burn and the orb vanish. Can't we relax now that the beast is gone? I'd like to enjoy the coming warmth. I can't believe Aurykk left his cave to rouse the sleeping dragons. Whatever for? They need their rest since all is peaceful again."

"Not for long, Alana. Rocánonom and Enderfon fear the beast's absence won't last. They're going to the Coldside Desert to find Haldoren, the third giant. They will bury him or revive him. He had great powers, too. If he lives, the three giants will fight the Malevir to the end."

"The Loblin say Haldoren died there, trapped in a spell. An aiglonax tore him apart and ate him...they said."

"The Loblin weren't there. How would they know he died?"

"Maybe they've seen his remains? I don't know. But tell me, why would the Malevir come back? Hasn't he seen we're too strong for him?"

"The Malevir wants the Mystic Scintilla."

"Why would the Malevir want to steal your fire and powers?"

"You know without them we dragons would lose everything. I think the beast is only hiding from us again, in a new way. Remember, Draako said he saw a strange specter escape to the orb."

"After the Elementals destroyed the tower?"

"Yes, and I dread to think it, but was that the Malevir who escaped to the orb, not consumed by fire, but waiting for renewed strength to destroy us dragons forever?"

Alana shudders and wraps her cloak tightly around her body despite the warmth of the afternoon sun.

"At least the amulet is gone and won't hurt any of us again."

"Yes, that is true. Meanwhile, we will be on our guard. But enough of this gloomy talk. Come, let us fly over the land. We'll visit Fossarelick and see how your brother is doing."

Alana jumps to her feet. She brushes dried grass and brown leaf crumbs from her cloak and, in a few easy strides, reaches Isabella's rider's hump. Settling in with the grace of long habit, she says, "It will be good to visit home again. Just like old times. Let's go."

www.ingramcontent.com/pod-product-compliance
Lightning Source LLC
Chambersburg PA
CBHW071550110726
47908CB00007B/2059